RETURN TO LILAC HILL

Joan D. Cooper

Copyright © 2014 Joan Cooper

All rights reserved.

ISBN 978-1-62806-038-6

Library of Congress Control Number 2014950443

Published by Salt Water Media
29 Broad Street, Suite 104
Berlin, MD 21811
www.saltwatermediallc.com

Cover Art by Stella Cunningham

This is a work of fiction. Names, characters, businesses, places events, and incidents are either the products of the author's imagination and/or used in a fictitious manner. Any resemblance to actual persons, living or dead, actual places or businesses, or actual events is purely coincidental.

DEDICATION:

"Every traveler has a home of his own, and he learns to appreciate it the more from his wandering."
— Charles Dickens

ACKNOWLEDGEMENTS:

Mary Jo and Amber--thank you for reading and encouraging.

A Lilac Hill Short Story 1

Eben Spence

1

In the distance, but out of sight, the unmistakable chainsaw buzz of a go-cart engine set Eben's teeth on edge. The little engine was quickly joined by the deeper-throated, coughing choke of a motorcycle. Refolding the half-read section of the Sunday news and picking up his coffee cup, Eben stood up and retrieved all evidence of a relaxed Sunday morning from the porch. Bad enough that he'd missed buying the little property next to his place, the loss stole his serenity. The small farm was barely visible through the narrow wilderness break of pines, sparse hollies and a few old oaks, but the new tenants came with a collection of noisy boys that he could hear.

They'd taken the old scooters, go-carts and motorcycles out of the back barn. One of the boys was obviously good at tinkering. When Eben toured the place months ago, none of the collection of rotted and rusty machines looked salvageable. Now they raced noisy, but unseen, all over the property at regular intervals after school and on the weekends.

It stuck in his craw that he'd missed buying the little

cherry spot of property that could further insulate his privacy. He'd missed the auction because his mother had a stroke the same morning. Lured to her deathbed in the next state, he'd sent an agent to the sale of the decrepit house, ancient barn and two hundred acres. Of course the bidding exceeded his expectations. Of course his tough, old mother hadn't died, so he was faced with the brats next door and bringing his mother home to live with him soon.

Eben couldn't, in good conscience, leave his mother in the home she'd drifted into following her neighborhood girlfriends who had all since died or moved in with adult children. She would need someone to help her while he worked during the day, so he would have to hire someone soon. He grimaced imagining the expense and the invasion of his solitude.

He'd bought this little slice of Lilac Hill long ago as a young man to leave the busy, little town and seek some quiet. Five years ago, the Monroe sisters had moved into the old Victorian farmhouse five miles away, but the abandoned buffer farm in between had kept them from little more than passing greetings. He liked those Monroe women because they were fiercely independent and went to work every day just like he did. The younger sister was a good accountant to refer to clients when he didn't care to mix business with personal finance.

Eben's eyebrows rose as a low, four-wheeled vehicle broke through the trees right at the edge of his property and careened wildly across the rutted grass. The rider tossed and flopped like a doll on a spring. Eben narrowed his eyes and stepped to the railing to get the go-cart in focus.

Eben Spence was off the porch and running toward his electric fence in a sprint as the go-cart tipped and raced in a wide arch toward his property line. Eben winced as it brushed the fence, and the little figure sprang as a jolt of the charge hit him. Gulping in the regret over his anger at the deer who had been feasting on his spring garden, Eben pulled himself up short, raced around to the barn and inside to yank down the kill switch for the fence. He glanced back out to the pasture and saw the sickening impact of the vehicle slamming into one of his hefty fence posts.

He picked up the receiver of the old landline in the barn and punched 911. He barely waited for the greeting of the operator and delivered the message, "This is Eben Spence out at Lilac Hill—15701 off Rt.16. Send an ambulance to my place—south pasture. Damn fool boy from next door just ran into my electric fence with a go-cart. He looked like he'd passed out before impact. Might have killed himself. Got that?"

The woman on the other end gave the affirmative. Everyone from nearby Lambertville and all the way up to Wheeling knew Eben Spence. The woman called for both the paramedics and the police figuring that if the person who was trespassing on Spence property wasn't dead already, he soon might be.

Claire got the call from Tony after the first of the after-church-services crowd had been served breakfast. She was actually surprised to hear his voice because the boys had been difficult to get out of bed since they'd moved to West Virginia. She wouldn't have been surprised to find them all still in bed when her shift ended at twelve. She'd left strict rules that forbade cooking after a forgotten, scorched pot last week and limited wandering outside because little Charlie had gotten lost on a ramble a few days ago. Claire looked at her frazzled reflection in the tall, walk-in freezer across from the phone and tried to excuse her slumped shoulders and wild-looking blond curls falling out of her chef's scarf as normal.

Between looking for a full-time job, unpacking the house, keeping the boys out of trouble and working this part-time cook position, Claire was at wit's end. "What's up Tony? I have another two hours on my Sunday shift. I'll bring home some of Gleason's sticky buns." The cooking job at Gleason's was a godsend after a few dead ends that had originally lured her to make a bid on the property outside the picturesque town.

She felt faint the moment she heard men talking and Charlie whimpering in the background. Tony took a hesitant breath. "You need to meet us. We're on the way to the hospital in Wheeling. Mom, it's Davey. We were fooling around with the go-cart, and it got away from him. I think he hit his head and then crashed into the fence. Can you meet us at the hospital?" Tony's voice was cracking. Claire could feel a rushing flood of panic filling her.

"Wheeling? Where is the hospital in Wheeling? I got a ride here this morning with Eddie. He's over at the hardware. I'll see if I can borrow Eddie's truck." She was just talking out loud like she always did in moments of disaster. With these three boys, the minor disasters were constant. This one sounded like the worst one since they'd moved away from Richmond.

Tony hurried on with a solution in which she could hear a bit of his father's steely voice. The command in his tone was chilling, "That's what I told old man Spence. He's the man whose fence Davey smashed. He's coming to get you; he's really mad and says he's pressing charges. But Mom? He was ready to do CPR and kept Davey still so they could check his spine, so don't let into him too much. Okay?" Tony's voice cracked like a boy's again. "Davey's coming around a little; see you at the hospital," and the line went dead just after she heard Charlie whine a bit more. The boys sounded really scared for a change.

Claire didn't even get a chance to take off her apron when a slam at the front door of the little café cracked, and Gleason's bellowed, "Claire? Get yourself out here! You have company!" Claire knew that sound. It was the sound behind the statement, "You're fired."

Picking up her purse, Claire also gathered her satchel of knives. She shrugged on her coat and picked up the extra sweater she kept with the coats figuring it might be gone by the time she got back. Mike Gleason, the large man who owned the place, was shaking his head and speaking to another man when she came through the double doors that separated the kitchen from the dining room. Claire frowned at the taller man speaking and gesticulating with large, bony hands. She had expected someone in his seventies, but if this was old man Spence, Tony must have an exaggerated idea of real age. "Old man Spence" might be older than she was, but this angry man was somewhere under fifty.

When the two men turned to face her, she shivered automatically. This was the man Tony was talking about? She had been turned down for a small business loan by this man the month after she'd used all her reserve cash to buy the farm. The banker had enjoyed delivering the bad news. His eyes narrowed on her small form, and a glint of amusement flittered through his eyes and teased over his mouth. "You're their mother! I can't believe I didn't connect it. Your boy Davey is in a bad way. I will take you to Wheeling—the littlest boy Charlie tells me you don't have your car."

Claire bristled and said, "I'll get a cab or something." Getting into a car with the unpleasant loan officer from the only bank in town was too much to bear. She reminded herself that Tony warned her to be civil. She didn't correct him when he named her their mother. Lots of people assumed that, and she'd grown tired of correcting them especially after the boys began calling her "Mom," so they didn't confuse little Charlie who had no memories of his real mother and only fragmented ideas of his father. It was laughable that anyone thought she was Tony's mother; at sixteen he had turned into a sapling who was probably six foot or more with dark whiskers that shadowed his cheeks in their new patchy growth every afternoon. If she'd been his birth mother, she'd have been an impossibly young fifth grader at the time of conception.

Eben Spence shook his head. "You're either going with me now, or I'll have you arrested for child endangerment. You can't leave three boys alone on a farm like yours. It's a wonder one of them hasn't been killed." He shook his head as Gleason made a little noise of protest.

"You're an overbearing pig. Tony is sixteen and more than capable of looking after them. How many children have you managed?" Claire's eyes filled with tears, and her cheeks grew hot from the avid interest among customers in the busy café.

Gleason tried to soothe her. "We know you're doing the best you can, Claire. Go with Spence. He's a mean, old man, but he'll get you to the hospital. It sounds like Davey is a bit roughed up. I'll ask Eddie to come and get you after the hardware closes." The big man patted her on the back and eyed the folded parcel with her knives stowed in the center. Gleason cocked a brow at the sweater tucked under her arm. He extended a hand for them, and Claire gave them up easily. "You will not be fired, Claire Reynard. You're the best cook I've hired in an age. Let me hold those for you. We can't have you dicing old Spence up in the next ten minutes when he inevitably acts like an ass again."

Eben Spence looked from the slight blond to the big man. "Dice me up?" He rocked back on his heels and grinned at the challenge this presented. So far, it had been one odd day.

Claire pressed her lips together for a moment and then walked out of the diner to wait for the gloating Spence outside. She heard her boss, Mike Gleason warn, "Her knives, Spence. You didn't believe me when I told you she was a bona fide chef, did you? I don't think you'd have a chance if you really pissed her off. Take care, old man. Thanks for taking her to Wheeling but lay off the righteous indignation act."

She felt the irritation in Eben Spence even as he came around in reflex and opened the door of his aged sedan, checked that her long coat wasn't in any danger and eased the creaky door closed. He was the oddest mixture of cranky, supposing ass and a perfect gentleman.

Trying to distract her attention from the grouch in the driver's seat, Claire looked at the old car's dash, at the wide uninterrupted seat and the antique safety belts. She hadn't seen a car like this since she was a little kid at car shows with her dad. Eben didn't waste the first few minutes speaking to her as he went through a series of automatic checks of the throttle, the pedals and the mirrors. He even adjusted the position of the huge, plush bench seat as if she'd magically moved it when she got in just a moment ago. He looked twitchy and nervous like a major league pitcher preparing to wind up into his best curveball. When he backed out of the spot at the diner, his right hand and arm draped over the seat back and came terribly close to her shoulder and cheek. She steeled her back straight but did not to flinch at the near touch.

As worried as Claire was about Davey, she recognized a number of facts as soon as she took a few calming breaths: Tony had called her, not the local or state police; at twelve, Davey was a child and would have been airlifted if his injuries were life-threatening; she had not been fired from her job at the café; the man beside her was a nervous wreck. The final fact made her oddly bemused; the old man both Tony and Mike Gleason had labeled this man Spence as was not so old at all. If he smiled, though it wasn't a likely occurrence, he could be ten brief years older like her brother Brian had been. But frowning at slower vehicles they passed and forcing the old car up over seventy miles an hour, he was thin-lipped, angry and definitely looked over fifty.

As they flew over the last mountain curve, Claire decided to try to speak to him. "Thank you for taking me to Wheeling. Tony told me you were the first one there for Davey." She flinched when he looked over at her.

He was coiled like a snake. "Couldn't have him dying on my place. What do you think you're doing on that farm? It's ridiculous—three boys and a woman on a place like that!" As she had calmed her nerves, he had been building his agitation with her. He shook his head. "You need a smaller place in town that you can afford. I did your paperwork myself before I turned down your loan request; you will declare bankruptcy by next year."

"Thanks for the vote of confidence." Claire's eyes flashed, and she decided that "old man Spence" was exactly the right label for him. No wonder he'd turned her down for the business loan. She wanted to defend herself and lash out, but she saw what he did. If she was honest, she'd admit that she had wondered the same thing from time to time. She thought of the boys in her cramped little house in

Richmond and winced. Then she pictured the small house in the town of Lambertville that her friend Julie had found for them to rent when they first moved. That tiny place hadn't worked either. Claire couldn't have predicted that the office manager's position at the mine would be cut before Claire could even start the job. The job with Gleason was part-time, but it paid living expenses, and the mortgage at the farm was almost paid in full.

Claire let go of a breath she'd been holding. Lambertville was a breath of fresh air after the congestion and pressure in Richmond. All of the money from selling her brother's Richmond townhouse had been dumped into the little farm on Lilac Hill. The military support payments for the boys kept them afloat beyond basic needs, but Claire hated to divert funds she was saving for the future. Three boys would quickly turn into three men who would need their college funds.

Her brother's estate was still in limbo with his missing person status overseas. The boys were her responsibility like they'd been full-time since Brian's wife had died just after Charlie was born. Brian promised this would be his last tour, but he had vanished during a firefight months ago. There had been an adventure every week that set her nerves on edge with three unruly boys who needed their father.

Eben Spence was filled with regret. He was not at home preparing the house for his mother's arrival, he was not finishing bank paperwork he had left for the weekend, and he was in the company of the most attractive woman he had ever wanted to spite in his life. She owned the property that he'd coveted for years to insulate his private compound completely from the outside world.

When he bought his five hundred acre place at twenty-six, his first act was planting trees along the outer edge for a fringy shield from public view. Extending the width of his farm another two hundred acres would have been ideal. He'd intended to raze the small house, rebuild the barn and play at raising sheep. During the auction, his agent hadn't wanted to battle with the other buyer though the price had climbed higher due to her impetuous bids. Eben knew she'd paid far too much, and he had been appalled that anyone had moved into the house without major repairs or renovation.

He cast a look in her direction and found her studying him. She had green eyes and blond hair like his mother. Eben ran a shaky hand through his own thick, graying blond hair and rubbed a bristly chin he hadn't bothered to shave with the excitement of the morning. He supposed she was comparing his disheveled appearance to his usual suit and tie at the bank.

She had looked hurt the day he'd turned down her loan application. She had stared at him for a long minute and nodded stoically. She must have been accustomed to adversity; she hadn't begged or groveled. She had asked for the name of his superior at the main office and examined him brutally. In a quietly lethal voice, she had asked, "This is rejection is personal, isn't it?" Her confidence made it obvious that she knew her credit was excellent.

Eben Spence had considered lying, but his conscience had forced a nod in her direction. "Odds are against you. Being from the outside, and trying to start a business? Your good credit in Richmond is a long way from here." He had nodded again as if she should understand that she was new to the area and no matter how glowing the recommendations, this was Lambertville, West Virginia. Eben Spence made up the rules of lending in this town.

They were winding into Wheeling through heavier traffic when she finally spoke, "Again, thank you for driving me all this way. I didn't realize before that we were neighbors, Mr. Spence. I didn't understand what was so personal about your refusing my request for a loan. I get it now." Her eyes were quick and fierce at his surprised laugh.

"I had no idea you'd bought the farm. The paperwork hadn't been processed." He raised an eyebrow in her direction, begging her to continue without another word.

She tapped her fingernail on the dash and angled her body to face him as he waited at a traffic light. "I thought you didn't like women. Or just me. You just don't want us on Lilac Hill, do you?"

Eben found his cheeks burning because she boiled it way so neatly. He now understood why she was not to be trusted with her set of knives and him in the car alone. The heat of her irritation with him was touching him from a few feet away. Why did he want it to escalate? He toyed with the idea that she was most interesting when angered. "Though it would make a nice plot, I didn't know who had bought the property or moved into the farm house. I was too irritated to look into it." This was a matter of ethics, and it burned in his cheeks. "I didn't know you were buying the place when I reviewed your business plan."

But he shrugged in the next moment which cemented her dislike of him. "I've wanted your little parcel of land for a long time. My mother had a stroke the day of the auction. That's the only reason your bid won the place. Why did you want to come here at all?" He did not like the fact that she'd become a person instead of a file folder with "declined" stamped on it.

Claire tried to clear her throat before she answered. In a roughened voice, she answered honestly, "To get the boys out of Richmond and give them a new start. They were grieving their father's absence and were starting down a bad path—at least Tony and Davey were. Charlie is too young to do anything more than follow the leader. Do you have any gangs here in Lambertville, Mr. Spence? Any huge drug problem? No, I didn't think so. And to set you straight, I will not be filing bankruptcy within the year. Get used to being our neighbor." She dismissed him before he could growl out a response by swiveling her knees to the front and staring out at the suburbs of Wheeling.

It was quiet in the old car for several minutes as Eben maneuvered through the highway interchange outside of the Wheeling city limits. He was thinking about the relief he'd felt when he realized the child was bruised up and limp but breathing. Eben had cut the engine by pulling the battery wire and lifted the go-cart off the boy who was sprawled in a sickening pile near the fence post. He'd been checking vitals by the time the older boy cut the engine and dropped the old motorbike.

Eben had been shocked at how calm and "take-charge" the older boy acted. He was tall enough to be mistaken for a man and acted like one as he knelt next to his little brother and said, "Davey? Hey, Davey, can you hear me? Don't move. Stay still."

Eben glanced over to the teary-eyed woman hugging the door of his old sedan. She was miles away inside worries. He had to hand it to himself; he was one mean, old cuss to rant at a pretty woman like her. Even in the bank the day he'd turned her loan request down, he had hesitated just a moment over her eyes, the glimpse of legs and a trim waist she showed off with a business suit. She'd had a smile he could elicit with just a bit of prodding even as he had turned down her application. He had enjoyed her dismay and irritation that day. Some little voice warned him that he'd pay for all that ill will he'd been building with this slight, pretty thing who didn't seem too delicate anymore despite her thin frame and the shadows under her eyes.

"What happened to their father?" Even he couldn't believe he'd asked it and gulped at the urge to fill in the blanks about the strange family. The boys were handsome children: Tony at sixteen, the unconscious middle one who was Davey at about twelve and the youngest boy Charlie who was perhaps seven. They were uniformly thin-framed, narrow-faced like her, but endowed with straight, dark hair and blue eyes. Eben glanced at her and inventoried curly blonde hair and green eyes sharpened like knives. Spence imagined their father must be a giant of a man with jet black hair, broad shoulders and the cool calm of the oldest boy who might tame the firebrand sitting in the car with him.

She sputtered, "Missing in action." She straightened at Spence's immediate throaty chuckle because she realized how it sounded. She growled, "No, you jerk!" Then she retorted, "Brian is a corporal in the Marines. He was stationed in the Middle East on his third tour. We received an official visit eight months ago—his company was hit, and they don't know whether he was taken or was killed. That's what missing in action means, Mr. Spence." She relented as she saw the sign for the hospital's emergency entrance. "Sorry for the attitude. People look at them and make assumptions. They are good boys; we are doing the best we can." Her eyes were blinded by sudden tears that fell despite her efforts to blink then back.

Spence rubbed his bristly chin and swore under his breath at the effect her words and her quiet tears created in his chest. He knew he should apologize for insinuating that her husband had run off from the trouble of the boys. He bypassed the main entrance and pulled into the parking garage. He decided not to abandon her to find her sons alone. He wasn't much for apologies, but he thought he might stay to see how the boy was and if they needed anything. If she was working part-time, there'd be no healthcare. Eben inwardly cursed at the urge to electrify the fence last year just to keep the deer in the woods and out of his fields.

Claire bolted from the car after he set the parking brake. He leaned across to lock her door as she strode across the short space to the elevator scanning the buttons for the emergency floor. He caught up to her as the elevator doors slid open. Her eyes were cold. "Thank you for bringing me, Mr. Spence. Eddie will pick us up after work. Please go home." She pressed the open button and gestured for him to step out of the car.

Spence shook his head, "No, I want to see how the boy is. If he's ready to come home, I'll take all of you back to Lilac Hill. I apologize for being rude to you. If you are going to be my neighbor, it would be best not to start feuding with you." His hair was beginning to stick out from running his hand through it in exasperation with his nerves. He finished his speech with logic, "Shame to have Eddie drive all this way when I'm already here." Inside his head, alarms were sounding at this gesture that begged her approval. Spence didn't usually care what other people thought about him.

Her eyes questioned a formerly relaxed, worn version

of the man in a battered flannel shirt and old denims. He wore ridiculous, corduroy loafers that he probably used as slippers around the house. This man had been caught by surprise and shanghaied out of his placid Sunday plans to help them out of a real mess. She nodded and lifted her finger from the button allowing the door to close.

She did not speak until the elevator jolted into rising. Her voice held apology, "Thank you, Mr. Spence. I know this has taken most of your day off." Tears were close again. "I am in your debt."

He nodded and rocked back on his heels as the elevator climbed to the right floor. Without true deliberation, words blurted out of him, "You don't have a full-time job yet, do you?"

The elevator raced past another floor as he considered. "Ever take care of anyone? Well, of course you have with the boys. How about someone older?" His eyes gleamed with the idea. "I was supposed to be fixing up rooms on the first floor today for my mother. She had a stroke and is moving home with me. I will be hiring someone for the daytime while I'm at the bank. Interested?" He felt a flush at his sudden impulsivity racing from his face to his neck. What had come over him?

She nodded very slowly. "I'll send over Tony to do any cleaning or painting you need done. He's an excellent handyman. Gets it from his dad." She blinked to understand and then stared right at him with that steely look again. "Work for you? You want me, a woman you threatened to report to Social Services not an hour ago, care for your mother?"

They left the elevator and hurried through the hallways and into the emergency waiting room. She heard Spence chuckle and mumble, "Well, I don't expect my mother will be riding any go-carts!" Claire choked back a laugh; even Eben was surprised the levity his words inspired. Again the thought occurred that she was the prettiest woman he'd spoken to in an age. He didn't correct her about the Social Services report. He had already complained to the responding deputies; they'd be in contact with the county office and start an investigation. Spence swallowed the thought and followed her through the maze of hallways and cubicles on the way to her son.

Davey was going to have a headache and vertigo for at least a week due to the concussion. The boys thought that he'd hit a tree limb as the cart careened out of control and raced through the thin screen of trees between the two properties. The doctors were initially concerned over the electric shock but concluded that the absence of burns on the boy meant that the frame of the cart had taken the brunt of the shock. Eben's report to the paramedics had insisted that the boy was breathing on his own though his breathing had been shallow. Eben had kept his mouth clear and hadn't moved him. Davey had escaped broken bones because he'd been limp when the cart upset and landed on him. There were bruises all over his body from the upsetting of the cart and jagged scrapes where skin had met bark, fence and ground. Eben watched Claire smooth back the boy's long bangs and speak to him quietly. She listened to the doctors, but a consultation with the child was the only thing that would satisfy her.

Her eyes glowed like coals when she looked at the oldest. She left Davey in the bed under Eben and Charlie's guard to march Tony out to the hallway for a face-to-face confrontation. Eben leaned out the door to spy on their conversation. He was weighing and measuring her handling of the boys. Eventually it would come out that he had complained to the responding officers and insisted that they file a Social Services report.

"I didn't mean for Davey to ride into the woods. We talked about staying in the old turnip field." Tony started his plea in a relieved, but exasperated tone like a parent might use.

She snapped, "We agreed. No machines operated without supervision. No exceptions." With her wild hair and fisted hands, she looked fierce as she bristled at his tone.

His voice rose on the defense, "I got up early and slipped out to the barn to work on the engine. You know I nearly had it running yesterday. I couldn't know that Davey and Charlie would get up and come out to the barn." He craftily tried to shift the blame away from himself.

Her voice was cold, "You are the oldest. If they followed you to the barn, all of you should have come back inside and watched some television until I came home. I have to work, Tony. I have to trust you to take care of them." She glared at him. "I guess I can't trust you to look after them. That episode in Richmond should have taught me, but you made promises. Should I hire somebody and sell the junk in the barn?" Tony's eyes must have bugged out because she waved a hand and lowered her voice. "Of course I shouldn't. You need to earn back my trust before you fiddle with any of that mess in the barn again. All the riding you'll be doing for now will be on the tractor to tend the fields. Are we clear?"

Watching her master this boy who was a few heads taller than her was sobering. She didn't cry or accept excuses. She had listened to his full report and gave him the terms of his repentance. He balked for many minutes as she hammered him with the cost of his actions. The boy finally nodded and looked back down the hall realizing that Eben and Charlie watched from a distance. Tony glowered and hunched his shoulders as they returned to the room.

Claire left them to speak to the attending physician and then called Eddie to stop him from driving into Wheeling. Eben cautioned the boys after she moved down the hallway with the doctor, "You three are lucky to have your mother. Stop giving her so much to worry over."

Tony snorted a laugh. "You watch your step, Mr. Spence. I have just been ordered to work with you nonstop until your mother moves in. It might not stop there. She's worried that we damaged your fence. I might actually be grounded until I join the Army when I turn eighteen." Tony rolled his eyes, but the other two boys gave Eben wide-eyed nods. "I knew starting up that go-cart was true stupidity this morning. We could have been watching TV and eating Gleason's cinnamon buns. Now I'm punished for life, and Davey might throw up for a week."

He quieted as he stared at his brother in the hospital bed who mouthed, "I'm sorry."

Tony grimaced and muttered, "I wish she'd stop bringing up Richmond." He looked at his brothers and admitted, "I have to stop pushing her buttons." He slumped into the only chair in the room and began to brood.

Eben felt like one of the boys in that moment, one of the men in this woman's male harem of willing if grudging, obedience.

2

When she started at the Spence house, Claire was overwhelmed between tending to Davey with his head injury, readying the Spence house for the arrival of Eben's mother, and creating a new schedule for the boys. She needed to balance working for Spence as his mother's companion during the day and keeping the evening hours at the diner in town.

She needed adult supervision for the boys even though both Tony and Davey were old enough to watch Charlie. A visit from the sheriff that included an interview of each Reynard had given her heartburn that lasted for days. Tony had a juvenile record in Virginia that was now common knowledge among law enforcement in Lambertville.

The deputy who took Tony's statement tried to ease her mind. "Most boys his age rebel, Mrs. Reynard." Clare looked at the man in uniform who did not look any older than Tony. Deputy Hanson was a bit full of himself but trying to comfort. "You've provided a stable home for them. You have good friends in the area, and Mike Gleason gave you a good recommendation. I'd make sure they're supervised while you're at work, but the accident could have happened when you were home. Don't worry." Claire had shaken her head at being chided by a man who might be ten years younger than her. The deputy looked barely out of high school.

For two weeks after the accident, she lived like a ping pong ball between the two farms with out of bounds shots into Lambertville to cook for Gleason. She had friends take the boys home, asked Eddie from the hardware to come a few evenings and called in sick twice at the diner when no adult was available. Claire was bone-tired but satisfied that life was beginning to resemble her normal but stressful existence.

During the third week, an odd but easy solution developed between Spence and the boys. One by one, they had accompanied the quiet man on all of his daily chores around the farm. He delegated a task to each boy depending on interest: machinery maintenance for Tony, care of the chickens to Charlie and weeding the rows of vegetables to Davey who had recovered quickly from the accident. Children were like that, she reflected once as she washed the dishes in her own kitchen while the boys played a loud game in the living room. They bounced back quickly while the adults around them stayed shell-shocked from the experience. Claire knew that she'd aged after this last episode.

One morning, Eben turned to Claire after he picked up his briefcase and offered, "I can keep the boys here each evening, Claire. After my mother settles for the evening, I'll walk them back and stay until you get home." He'd glanced out the window to the pasture he imagined walking with the boys. He'd need to build a gate in the fence where the old path through the woods cut through the two properties.

Claire had sputtered and wrung her hands in the apron she donned every morning as a routine. "That's too much, Mr. Spence. I'm looking for a regular sitter or someone who would like to rent a room. I thought I could barter a room for supervision—something like that. Not everyone wants to live in town."

His brows had risen as he listened to her nonsensical plan. "Invite a stranger to live with you? Bad enough you are out here with three boys alone." His voice was too hard. He'd meditated on Claire and the boys in the dilapidated house and wondered if the furnace was safe, if the water still ran rusty or if the wiring was frayed inside the aged walls. Parts of the house were nearly one hundred years old, but he doubted she knew that.

Claire had snapped, "It's none of your business, Eben Spence."

His mother made a strangled sound of dismay from her chair in the kitchen, so they both turned. Her finger was tracing words on her tray in the colored sand the therapist was teaching her to use. "NO FIGHTING," was boldly formed though it slanted in the direction of her list to one side. The old woman's eyes pleaded with them.

Eben changed tactics. "I need the boys here, Claire. Davey has started reading a book my mother likes. He told me that he has to read for thirty minutes a day, and she enjoys it. And Charlie asked me to help him with long division. I can find work for Tony." He was logical and cold, but his even tone put her at ease.

"If you need them." He watched her eyes seek out his mother's face for approval. Claire's face softened as the two women communicated silently.

Eben nodded. "I'll expect them to stay this evening." He was out the door and rushing out to the garage before she could whisper the thanks that she uttered to herself.

Lizzie Spence quickly became more like a friend than an invalid recovering from a stroke. Lizzie's eyes were bright with intelligence though her words were garbled from paralysis on the left side of her body. Claire drove her to the occupational therapist twice a week and took over repetitions of the exercises for the days between visits. She noticed that Lizzie was improving in her interactions with others, especially her conversations with the boys and Eben.

The old woman rarely sat in a room without some focus for her attention, whether it was Claire cleaning the house or cooking, the boys squabbling through homework, a television program about history or Eben working the farm.

With some prompting, Lizzie was trying to use the exercises from the therapist to regain limited use of her left side and to strengthen her dominant right.

The absence of further word about Brian lulled Claire into routine. After Davey healed and Liz Spence was set into a routine of physical therapy and rest, the only thing Claire found taxing were the long hours because the shift at the diner lasted until ten. She often sleepwalked through her shift at the diner and arrived at the house on Lilac Hill without any memory of the trip from the diner to the farm.

3

During her first month working for him, Claire discovered that Eben Spence had a secret reading habit that tickled her immensely. She noticed the little paperback books tucked into various corners of the house on her first few forays into keeping his house. Mostly they were westerns and some histories, but Eben Spence also enjoyed romances. Claire tried not to disturb their nested presence in the house. After two weeks watching the volumes move and disappear, she filched one and began to read it after her evening shift at the diner. She stayed up until one in the morning absorbed in the lurid adventure. She eyed the trim figure of the tall man when she relieved him the next morning and wondered about his penchant for light literature.

One slow night at the diner, she asked one of the waitresses if she had ever dated Eben. The older woman giggled and said, "No, not my type." They grinned at each other because, even with her hair going gray and her boobs sagging, Sally Hilligoss dated everything in pants that expressed interest.

Claire's boss Mike had winked at both women. "Maybe Eben hasn't met the right girl yet." Mike Gleason covertly watched Claire digging for information on the town loner and finally teased her, "Are you interested, Claire?"

She just shook her head at that little jab and waved a large knife in the big man's direction. "Don't go there, Mike." Claire began taking one of the little books home with her each day in a bag that she carried everywhere. She dreamed of the alpha-male heroes and the damsels in distress instead of her constant worries about money, the boys and her missing brother for the first time since high school. Sometimes she took a history book and filled in blanks in her education, but she enjoyed the romances much more.

While she was cooking, Claire let her mind wander and puzzle over how many times she imagined that the heroes looked like Eben. He did have thick, wavy blonde hair that was beginning to thread white instead of steely gray. There was a cleft in his chin and his lips were often thin with disapproval when he spoke to her. She grinned at the nonsense, but she knew there must be more than imagined muscles under those baggy shirts he wore at home or hid beneath his business suits. He did all the outside work on his place and hired out only for the final harvest of wide swath of soy greening his south fields. He'd put the boys to work on the kitchen garden he kept in the back, and he had offered to pay them by the chore.

He and Claire avoided each other most of the time like a pair of wary dogs. No matter what he thought of her, Eben wasn't disapproving with the boys. He laughed at their antics and often challenged them to verbal duels. They were beginning to take on real chores at home now that he walked them back to her farm after his mother settled in her room every evening. He was usually sitting on Claire's front porch when she pulled up in her little car after her shift at the diner. Sometimes she brought him home an extra slice of pie or cake. Claire grimaced at her daydreaming; he was a bit thin, but there must be a strong man under the habitual loose shirts and cotton trousers. Eben Spence always looked proper and buttoned up even in worn, casual clothes.

Eben discovered that she'd been borrowing the little books after he found a familiar paperback in her bag one afternoon. He'd had decided to change her windshield wipers and fill the washer fluid after Tony complained about the wipers. The boy was taking driver's education at school and had become unaccountably snotty about the condition of Claire's old sedan. Eben gave the boy the number for the blades and had walked with him after school to buy them from the auto parts counter at the hardware. Eben figured that if Tony was going to drive, he'd better be ready for minor maintenance.

When Eben reached inside for her keys to the car, he touched and then extracted a well-worn paperback. He frowned at it and then slid it back inside. The next afternoon, the same book was back on top of the jelly cabinet in the pantry.

In a state of mild alarm, Eben watched her take and replace the little books. One evening after she'd left the boys in his care, he settled each of them with homework, checked to see if his mother was occupied, and began removing each paperback from its tucked spot.

After collecting over thirty in less than ten minutes, Eben began to chuckle as he removed little notes sticking out of each one. "Dream man," one said. Another quipped, "No woman is that helpless!" He stopped removing them from the pages when he spotted "Ridiculous dialogue during sex. Is that possible?" He opened it and read the scene all the way through and remembered thinking the little book was a simple excuse to string together a series of lurid encounters between the main characters.

The thought that Claire had read it and imagined him reading it made his ears go bright red. He gathered the little paperbacks in a cardboard box and carried them up to his study. She didn't often go in there by some unwritten agreement between them.

He selected one that looked untouched and left it on the kitchen counter for her with a note that said, "Guilty pleasure." When he returned that evening, he found the book she had borrowed the night before and a bent copy of Pride and Prejudice with a responding note. "Herein find the original alpha male grappling with no shrinking violet.

Lizzie is much more interesting than the usual limp flower." He shook his head and replaced her volume with his favorite Bronte Jane Eyre with a note that said, "Touché! Jane is neither violet nor alpha. She is much more interesting than the broody, wooden Rochester."

Claire had laughed out loud when she read it. The next morning, she rushed into the house before he could disappear up the road on the way to the bank. He came into the kitchen and let her straighten his collar as he examined the curl of her hair and the quirky eyebrow that told her interest in him.

He asked the only question that popped into his head concerning literature with her lips so close to his, "So is it pride or prejudice between us, Claire?"

She smiled and cocked her head to the side and answered, "Definitely prejudice on your part, Mr. Spence. I believe you told me I was an outsider the first time we met!" She raised her eyes to dare him to deny his words.

He shook his head and thought that she should not let pride rule her; it might be her downfall. He brushed his lips on her forehead before he stepped away to pull on his jacket and leave for work.

4

Social Services made Claire cry. That was Davey's conclusion when he reported her crying jag to Tony and Charlie during their brothers' meeting before she arrived home from their case review. There had also been an official-looking letter from the Marines waiting all afternoon on the foyer table.

Tony had the worst desire to call Mr. Spence because he was even-tempered, and the older man looked at Claire like she was something fragile when they were all together. Tony was used to men looking at Claire like she was something they could grab up and eat. Now that he was a nearly a man with grown man urges, he understood that Claire was like some wonderful dessert that many men wanted to savor with her curly, blond hair and wide, green eyes. Tony felt guilty for looking, but he admitted to himself that his Claire had a figure and curves that made men wonder. Mr. Spence looked at her and emitted pride tinged with a bit of fear; Tony appreciated the difference because he admired her in a similar fashion.

Tony didn't hesitate to call. "Mr. Spence? Can you leave your mother for a few minutes? Mom is late coming back from the Social Services hearing, and there's a letter or a telegram here. From the Marines." Eben listened to the earnest concern in the boy's voice and understood the machination he'd set in motion during his initial reaction to Davey's accident; his first, ill-spoken words to the police had finally reared back in ugly repercussions.

Claire looked exhausted and dusty from driving home with the windows open when she sank down on the front steps to open the sealed telegram. The boys and Eben hovered in the background while she read it a few times. On top of an investigation by Social Services that exposed her to microscopic inspection, the Marines had found DNA evidence of Brian Reynard on a charred, roadside battle site with a number of other fallen servicemen. After ten months missing in action, Brian had been declared dead. She had a service to organize in Richmond where their leftover family still resided and a formal hearing before a Social Services commissioner about the accident at the farm.

After even Tony sobbed broken-heartedly, the boys were put to bed like they were toddlers. Eben sat with Claire on her front porch and watched the moon move slowly across the sky. She seemed too stoic about this new loss. He actually dared to hold her for a few minutes, so she could lean on his chest and let her head rest on his shoulder.

She rubbed her forehead and whispered, "I hope he didn't have pain. I hope it was fast." There was a catch in her voice, but Eben figured she had decided her husband was gone a long time ago. She surprised him by brushing a kiss on his cheek and giving him a little hug of an embrace, "It doesn't feel real; I think I would know if he was dead."

She stared up at the stars and spoke unconsciously, "I remember the first time I met Brian. My mother had been dating this very scary, big man for months—he was very friendly towards me, but he was so tall and imposing. On the night they took me out to tell me they were getting married, this handsome young man dressed in a uniform joined us at the table halfway through the meal. He had a glower that stopped my heart. I think I fell in love with him on the spot—puppy love—I was only seven, and Brian was twenty-two. Anthony Reynard made my mother so happy. I thank God that they had each other. They died in a car accident fourteen years later during a trip through the mountains. Single car. I came home from college and found out that Brian's wife was sick, and he was out on maneuvers. She died a week after we plowed through red tape and brought him home."

Her rambling discourse had sobered him. She wasn't their mother, he realized and chided himself for avoiding the mathematics of Tony's age or digging back into her bank file for Claire's true birthdate. Yet she was their mother in every sense but biology. She carried the weight of her charges with the air of a much older woman. She didn't wear makeup to hide crow's feet or lines about her mouth. When she laughed, she did so out loud and cried in the same way.

"How old are you, Claire?" She was a warm weight against his chest. He angled his head to feel her soft hair against his cheek.

"Nearly thirty. Can you believe it? I'd just turned twenty-one when Charlie was born. I left the university with two semesters to go because I added a major." She caught up with Eben's thinking, "How old are you, Eben Spence?"

"Forty-four this January. Too old for you, but you are too young to be living this life, Claire." Eben didn't care what she said about years or maturity; his heart was racing at having this warm woman resting in his arms. He molded her into his body and kissed her to unthinking blinks. Eben had not even realize he knew how to thoroughly kiss a woman like that until Claire eased into his arms. They were a terribly good fit, his gut told him.

Later in bed, he rubbed bristly cheeks and worried his beard might have burned her skin. He went to sleep thinking about those kisses for a week.

Three months later during an unannounced visit, David Elliott, the Social Services agent from the Wheeling office, found the boys tending to chores and homework while Claire finished dinner preparation at the Spence house. No one but the dog had been home at Reynard place, but the Spence house was full of noise and bustle. Homework was strewn on a big table on the front porch, and a man's suit jacket was draped over the banister in the front hall. David heard the sound of Claire, Lizzie and Charlie laughing over potato peels in a steaming kitchen, and he found Eben Spence bent over a table in the backyard with the parts of a science fair project that wild-haired Davey was trying to assemble for the next day. Tony had greeted the man at the gate with garden shears in one hand and a bag of garden trash in the other. Tony looked taller and more filled out since the agent's first visit after the accident.

The report of the accident was still troubling. Claire's lack of full-time employment in the little town was even more so. The man wanted to find out exactly who was minding the boys while she worked her late shift at the diner.

David Elliott looked at the file and asked, "Who watches the boys when you're working? A few months ago, it sounded temporary."

Claire pushed her frizzy hair back and gestured for David to go into the living room. Charlie had looked worried. "They stay with Mr. Spence when I go to the diner in the evening. We worked out a permanent arrangement."

"Eben Spence?" The young man frowned and pushed his glasses up, "Mr. Spence was the person who reported you. You now list him as an employer."

Claire glared at Michael Elliott and Eben Spence who had rushed into the house when Charlie alerted him. She wanted to feel annoyed or betrayed, but Claire also knew that Eben had made the complaint in the heat of the moment. She understood his grouchy desire for solitude that he'd been robbed of by his mother's stroke, Claire's high bid on the property adjoining his, and his own impetuous offer to help with the boys. Claire understood that she needed to provide the boys with a male role model. Eben Spence was a good man despite his old man grouchiness, his penchant for romance novels, and miserly attitude toward bank loans. He was a good man with exceptional morals.

Claire said, "Agent Elliott? This is Eben Spence. I think we've solved our differences since our first, awkward meetings. The boys have supervision twenty-four hours a day. Please put that in your report."

Spence nodded and returned to the porch to oversee the rest of Davey's homework. His heart banged in his chest.

Claire and the agent discussed the report at the dining room table. Elliott had labeled Claire Reynard "young, struggling and overwhelmed—too proud to use the death benefit from the government for living expenses. Excellent caregiver if challenged decision-maker." David Elliott confided that he'd file a report saying that she needed monitoring and counseling, but overall, the boys were safe with her if she disclosed a plan for supervision while she worked.

He'd eyed the rebellious sixteen-year-old and frowned over the bad decisions that led to the middle child's go-cart adventure. Anthony Reynard seemed a handful of willfulness. There were no indications that he had continued the previous pattern of truancy and destruction of property after the move to Lambertville. Tony's teachers had given glowing reports of his work habits and achievement.

Spence rose from his porch rocker after the visit from the social worker and approached Claire who dabbed at her eyes in the living room. The boys had come in to find out what Social Services might demand, and Charlie had pushed Lizzie's chair into the room. Claire could be brave when faced with adversity, but she became emotional just after.

The boys were accustomed to her teary response, but Eben was concerned. He hugged her gently as she sniffled. His voice was low, "I apologize for making that complaint. Please forgive me." He cast a hand down her back to comfort her.

She closed her eyes and sighed, "I'd have done the same thing in your place, Eben."

He tightened his arms and offered, "If you married me, I'd be their legal guardian; I'm here every afternoon and evening. My mother loves the boys like grandchildren. That would be permanent enough, wouldn't it?" Eben's voice revealed no thought of romance, but his eyes glittered with longing.

Claire eyed Eben's proposal of marriage, offered like a protective business deal or a bank loan. Claire had frowned at him, "What kind of crazy idea is this? Life is no romance novel, Eben." Then she bristled, "Do you understand what you're getting with this gesture? We're a big package deal—a stubborn woman and three boys." She tried to make her tone light, "Maybe you still want my farm?"

Lizzie Spence had protested by falling into a sideways slouch and emitting a little groan of pain which distracted Claire. The old woman's eyes had been streaming tears since the beginning of the tense meeting.

Dabbing at the old woman's face, Claire missed the stab of pain in Eben Spence's face as he heard her harsh acceptance of his offer. He'd thought she'd figured out how much he enjoyed the boys with their noise, troubles and nonsense. The Reynard boys had interrupted and tossed his quiet life into tumult.

Eben thought that Claire had realized how much he enjoyed her. So he made a joke of it and drawled, "Come on, Claire. Let me be the stereotypical banker in the old western who marries the girl for her inheritance. It would be good for my reputation in town."

Claire growled at him, "You'll need to break that mold. The mean banker always winds up losing the girl and the farm." She rolled her eyes at their ridiculous answer to the problems of the boys.

He didn't know that the furnace had stopped working again, and she'd had to turn off the water in the back part of the house that morning with the first of the deep freezes likely in the next few days. She had spent the day trying to figure out what to sell to buy a new furnace. She had finally spoken to Tony about using some of the funds from his father's account for repairs. She regretted the germ of unease in her heart, but relented, "Yes, Eben Spence, I'd like to marry you."

5

They were married in the Lutheran church he'd attended once a week since birth. The whole town came out to see Lambertville's elusive bachelor marry the most accomplished cook that Gleason had ever hired at the diner. Eben told everyone that his mother walked down the aisle on Tony's arm strictly because of Claire's determined work with Lizzie. The boys stood at the front of the church with Eben as she walked down the aisle on her uncle's arm.

Claire had a few cousins and a pair of uncles in attendance, but her side of the church was full of diner staff, customers and friends of the boys from Lambertville and Richmond who could drive there with the short notice. Two of Brian's friends from high school attended looking somber and delivered a few boxes that contained the rest of the man's belongings from storage.

Eben had pretended not to care about the service or the reception that Claire and Mike Gleason had honed into a spreading picnic under tents beside Eben's fine house. The air was chilly in late October, but the changing colors in the trees adorning Lilac Hill made a beautiful backdrop. When he visited the tables with his bride who seemed to know everyone, Eben felt warmth invade his chest. It was the same feeling he got when he closed a good business deal.

He was surprised to see the Elliott man from Social

Services at his neighbor's table. The sisters from Monroe Farm held court at a table populated with raucous, childish noise from their collected progeny and husbands' families. Michael and Julie Elliott stood to embrace Claire and congratulated Eben with wide grins. Michael slyly spoke to Eben, "My brother here says you moved fast and snapped Claire up. Good going." He gestured to the suddenly embarrassed David Elliott to whom Claire was giving a smiting look. "I've been running off a few of those suitor-types who'd been nosing around her."

He gestured toward the primarily young, unattached men who laughed together near the open bar. "I've known Brian Reynard's family for years—good people. I was the one who suggested the farm when it came up for auction because it was so close to our place. I didn't know you wanted it so badly, Mr. Spence. But looking at the two of you with those boys, I'd say you owe me."

Spence eyed the man whom he usually viewed as a poor credit risk but personable and easy to like. He found himself nodding as Claire tugged at his hand and led him to the next table. It was all good if he held onto her hand.

The next morning when she moved into his bedroom, she played it like a bit of comedy. He'd shown her the guest bedroom next to his that she might want for privacy. She had put her hands on her hips and frowned. She colored a bit to show she did not speak this frankly on a regular basis with anyone. "Look Eben. I understood about the wedding night because we had two houses full of people and a handful more at Monroe Farm. Even the boys had folks rooming with them. It wasn't all that romantic." She tapped a foot because he was knotting his tie for work and absorbed in examining her agitated figure instead of his habitual neat knot.

He had the worst desire to clear up her worries over his attraction to her and go in late to work. The boys were headed into town on school busses, and his mother was distracted with the television news in the front parlor. It was irritating that they were never free of other people.

Claire had on a thin, frayed cotton blouse over slim jeans that morning. Eben glanced at himself in the dresser mirror and saw that the knot of the tie was a mess, as he considered her pastel, loose clothing. She was waiting for a response. "Come here, Claire. Help me untie this mess." Whether it was the silk at his throat or every tension in his body, who cared?

She crossed the room and unknotted the tie. She unbuttoned his crisp shirt and pulled it off of him. She handed him the phone and said, "Call out, Eben. I'll get something pretty on . . ." but she stopped speaking when he hauled her against his chest.

"You are just fine like that, Claire. Taking this blouse off of you is all the pretty I want." Eben's throat ached. He gestured for her to make the call. "Tell my secretary I need a day for my honeymoon."

Claire rolled her eyes, speed-dialed the bank and asked for his secretary. "Mr. Spence won't be in today. He's coming down with something. He'll call you later, okay?" She hung up the phone and watched her husband empty out half his dresser into a laundry basket and gaped as he pushed his careful suits over to one side of the closet. "Could you fit your things into that much space?"

He raised an eyebrow as she nodded without protest because he'd heard that women came with loads of extra belongings. His mother had returned from her apartment with two houses worth of boxes, but Claire was streamlined like her sparse collection of fine knives. She was back to looking in the dresser mirror when he came behind her to rest his large hands at her waist. "So you want to be my wife?"

Claire gave a bit of a nod. "I married you, didn't I? I want to rest against you in the dark, Eben Spence. I want us to lean on each other." Reflected in the old mirror, he saw her extreme youth at twenty-nine to his forty-four years. He examined their blond hair one shade apart—hers curly and his thick and wavy. He looked at the dapper beard he'd worn since he could shave that was touched with gray in places just like his temples. He looked too uptight for the vibrancy resting against his chest. She was endued with light and youth.

He glanced up again and watched his hands fumble at her buttons and zipper. Once his fingertips found skin, he moved on impulse and instinct. He figured it might take a lot of practice to learn to lean. He was amazed at their tight, hot fit and the soft sounds she made when she let herself lose the tension in her body. Eben Spence wondered over waiting for this woman to arrive all the days of his life.

6

Claire was suddenly in the doorway to his office less than a year after he'd met her there and tried to squash her hopes. He looked up and was struck in the chest by how unconsciously beautiful his wife looked in her casual clothes and without a touch of makeup. She was bursting with some news, but Eben wanted to hold her tight and gobble her up right there in the bank.

"Claire?" His voice caught because just behind her towered a large, older man-sized version of Tony Reynard wearing a slight frown and the straightjacket of a uniform showing he was Marine of rank.

Blushing, she glanced down as an electric look flashed between the two men that told the story, "She's mine; you can't have her back," to the new man's thunderous growl, "No way in hell." They were immediately bristling and growling like territorial wolves.

Claire pulled the man in the uniform into the office and explained, "Brian, this is my husband Eben Spence." Her eyes met Eben's with a silent, baffled question, "Eben, Brian surprised me at the house—there was a terrible but wonderful mistake. Brian was rescued from an Afghan rebel cell a few days ago. He just arrived home with a friend; can you believe it?" She had begun crying though she still smiled. Eben figured it was the enormity of finding herself caught between two men who were strangers.

Brian Reynard was still in the scowling mode. He extended his left hand, and Eben took it awkwardly. The right sleeve was empty and pinned to the shoulder of the uniform jacket. Eben felt the absence of the limb as if he was a casualty of chance. Eben left the office that day to walk down the street to the lower school and reunite Davey and Charlie with their father. Eben felt his heart slow in degrees; his life was going dark because Claire would certainly be going back home with Brian.

"Why are you still here? I thought you you'd be going back to the house with Brian and the boys." Eben rocked back and tried to look casual, but his heart was hammering in his ears. She'd just come into the bedroom with an armload of clothes and had given him a bashful smile. It had been one long and trying day.

Claire looked like he had slapped her; the irritated, old man Spence was back, and he was very unfriendly. She shook her head and said, "Eben, no matter the reason at the beginning, we are married. Do you want me to leave you?"

He said nothing in shocked gladness that she assumed she should stay. "Your mother and I get along well," she offered lamely as she finished putting away his underwear and socks in the top two drawers of the dresser.

His eyes slid over to her side. Six months married to her left him with no memory of what he'd ever housed on her side of the dresser. He'd used it since he was twenty-two years-old and returned home with an advanced degree in finance. The bedroom set had been his grandparents' set ordered straight from France. Claire didn't overwhelm him with things as he'd feared she might. She slid into the space he'd given her. The boys had done the same and had been respectful of his accustomed quiet after they had moved into his house.

The wind had been bone-aching cold on the day they winterized her farmhouse and moved the boys into his big house. She had guiltily revealed that the furnace had stopped working the day he proposed. He was in awe of her honesty as she revealed the bare truth of her avarice over a warm home for her children. He hadn't even blinked over calling the oil company and ordering the new unit. He'd hired an electrician with the next call to inspect and replace all of the wiring.

His mouth watered thinking about the first morning he'd woken to her warm body in the bed beside him. How had he weathered all these changes so easily? It was all Claire.

He'd been sitting on the bed rereading their prenuptial agreement because he assumed she'd go home with her brother. What woman would not go home with the large, handsome man who was even more vital without his right arm than the pictures in the boys' old album? Brian was likeable just like his boys were. They were family.

Eben felt a different stab of regret over their leaving his big house. The front hallway seemed to echo tonight in their absence. He assumed Claire would just glide right over the fields between the old Spence place and the new swath of land people were beginning to refer to with the Reynard name. He figured that she would gladly rest in her own bed tonight and then remember old Eben Spence in the morning. But she was there putting clothes away and quizzing his words in confusion.

"Do you want me to go?" Biting her bottom lip, she asked, "Do you want some time alone?" There might be a little shimmer of moisture in her eyes. "Am I too clingy? Do I crowd you?"

He choked over answering. He shook his head.

She came forward, as she unbuttoned her blouse to look down at what he was reading. When she recognized it as the prenuptial, she smiled faintly. "Are you getting ready to shuck me off, Eben Spence?" Her eyes shone with brimming tears, but she blinked them away. She flicked them off her cheeks with two fingers in annoyance.

She sat down on the bed to face him but continued to loosen her blouse. She examined his serious expression and slightly downcast eyes. She edged as close to him as she could without touching him; she gained his full attention.

His voice was back to his grouchy, old man growl, "You have been very sweet to me, Claire. My mother loves you, and I appreciate how well you care for her. She's improved far more than the doctors expected, but I can't hold you to this marriage. Brian is home now. You don't really need me anymore, do you?"

"What I need? I don't think my place is anywhere but with you, Eben Spence!" Claire sighed and reached over to the papers on the bed and folded them neatly to slip them back into the lawyer's envelope. She tossed the envelope on the floor and huffed out a breath at his raised eyebrows.

She leaned forward and began unbuttoning his shirt. He complied with this coercion by slipping her blouse down her arms, so he could look at her in her thin camisole and bra. The woman wore layers of clothing that made it a pleasure to reveal her slowly before bed every evening. He traced a rough thumb over one shoulder and leaned forward to lower his mouth to her bare skin. Her whisper told hurt, "You would let me go so easily, Eben? You wouldn't even try to keep me?" Her eyes filled with tears again. She shivered when his beard touched her skin.

He had begun to smooth her straps away with his fingers and his mouth. He didn't want to say it, but he felt her dragging the words out of him, "I love you, but you told me you loved Brian Reynard." Humor crept back, and he looked her in the eye, "Really Claire, I think he could beat the crap out of me without trying."

She was already into a dreamy zone she slipped right into when they got ready for bed together. She had somehow unzipped her jeans and done the same for him. She made him feel like a god with her little siren's wriggle over losing her clothes.

Her hearing must have been on some kind of delay. She was down to a bra and panties before her head snapped up. She froze in a crouch over him. Her eyes flashed just like months ago when he realized how dangerous she might be with knives. Her eyes glittered over him. "Brian? Of course

I love him. Like a brother," she sat up, knelt beside him and stared. "And I thought that I as the innocent, romantic one in our pair. Geez, Eben! Do you want me to leave you?"

She grinned as he looked away and blushed. She leaned down and whispered, "Brian is my step-brother. Those boys belong to him even though you and I will miss them. But I am your wife now. You are stuck with me."

Eben's eyes were wide as the shock that she was truly his to keep washed him. Gratitude and a bit of awe replaced the shock as she slipped under the covers and leaned against him. He raised his left arm and hugged her closer fingering the remains of her clothing. "You are the only woman I have ever loved," Eben admitted. "Come here, Claire."

He pulled her close to unknot her tension. He could deal with the truth later. He didn't need to figure out relationships outside theirs that evening between her lovely body, which he'd thought he'd lost, and then complete exhaustion. She heard him as she drifted off to sleep. "Please don't leave me, Claire. I," he hesitated, and she knew how awake he really was, "I do love you. I don't want you to go."

Claire rolled over to her side and nestled into the place where she fit against him and murmured, "I am right where I belong, Eben. And I love you back." She fell into sleep with a slight grin on her face.

7

Tony was the first of the boys to move back into Eben Spence's house. The tall, dark-haired boy approached Eben at work. He sat in the waiting area while Eben met with Joseph Lambert to open a trust account for his daughter's new baby. Eben watched Joseph Lambert bluster over the trust; families were complicated. Eben had never faced his avoidance of the messiness of a family. Claire and the boys had thrust the chaos of family onto him at the same time his mother had needed him. He saw it all as a convergence of the twain just like some devastating world war. He had gained so much from this particular war that he was becoming overconfident with it.

Joseph Lambert cleared his throat and brought Eben's mind back to business. The young woman, Sarah Monroe Stone, was resistant to the idea of Joseph giving her child any of the Lambert inheritance. He'd recently acknowledged the woman as his daughter and had added her name to his will. His son Jason Lambert had shared the story with Eben over a beer one evening; the drama of Sarah's refusal to acknowledge Joseph's claim on her was wrapped up in her dogged devotion to the man who had raised her. Jason and his brother were fond of their half-sister, and their mother Isabel Lambert had had welcomed Sarah with enthusiasm. Sarah contended that she didn't care about DNA and the like; her father was still the man who raised her as his own.

Eben glanced out to the stormy boy waiting to see him and thought that sometimes nurture was preferable over nature. Claire was more of a parent to Brian's three boys than their father had been for the past seven years. Claire had the caretaker tendency that allowed the needs of the boys supersede her own.

Eben felt he was lucky that she hadn't fought that natural inclination with his mother. Lizzie Spence was becoming more vital every day; his mother had helped with the dinner a few nights last week and had taken up her needlework again. Claire, she said, was a good knitter who'd shared a few of her projects. Eben had concluded that Claire might be excellent at anything she put her mind to study. He understood that she had studied him and decided to master him in steadying increments of attention, affection and lavish unselfishness. He was lucky he hadn't managed to frighten her away.

Joseph Lambert tried to make further conversation about Jason and his flirtation with the woman Sarah had lured to the town to work with her at the Monroe sisters' accounting firm. In another time, Eben would have felt bothered by the waiting boy and continued the mindless talk. Eben stood and extended his hand to Joseph and said,

"The trust is easy enough to create. If you have the baby's social security number, we can set it up. I'll see Jason at the social on Sunday. I have another client waiting today."

He gestured to the seated boy and beckoned for Tony to come and meet Joseph Lambert. "Joseph, I'd like you to meet Anthony Reynard. He is Claire's nephew. Tony, this is Joseph Lambert. Mr. Lambert is a good friend and lives on the other side of the mountain from your farm. His daughter Sarah and her sister Julie own Monroe Farm just next to yours."

Tony nodded and gave Joseph a level look. "I thought Miss Sarah was the pastry chef for the Lamberts at Lilac Hill Research. Your daughter works for you?" His eyes widened as he looked from Eben to Joseph. "She mentioned you might need another grounds man. I was going to apply." There was an edge of distrust in Tony's eyes. Eben realized that something had made him wary of Joseph Lambert.

Joseph smiled and patted the boy's arm. "Sarah does not like to admit I'm her father, but it's true. Yes, she is one of our chefs, and I think you should apply if you need a job close to home." Joseph nodded to both of them and left.

Eben frowned at Tony because the serious boy wore the gravity of his worries in his dark eyes. A new stiffness forced his shoulders down. Eben waved him into the office and into a chair before the desk. Instead of slipping behind the desk, Eben moved another chair opposite Tony, so they could talk like they were on the front porch together. "You wanted to speak to me?" He expected a request for a loan of some sort; Eben was a banker, and the boy sat in the bank which was the oldest brick building in Lambertville. Eben had always enjoyed the stately deportment of the place set like a jewel on a busy corner in the center of town. He glanced around and wondered if Tony found it awe-inspiring.

Tony nodded and asked, "Why did you become a banker?" He looked away at the large desk with the neat piles of paperwork and stuttered, "That's not why I got off the school bus early, but I'm curious." He tried to grin at Eben.

At the moment the question hit him, Eben had

straightened in his seat. No one had ever questioned his decision to follow his father into management at the bank. His great-grandfather had opened the branch when the town of Wheeling was an outpost on the way down to the southern cities or out to Ohio and beyond. Eben had never thought beyond improving the services and profitability of their institution. It was expected from the only son. Eben narrowed his eyes and let Tony down just a bit, "It was expected; I am good with numbers and logic. The job fits me. Why?"

Tony shrugged and confessed, "I have been telling myself all my life that following my Dad into the Marines or even the Air Force like my granddad would be natural. It's all I ever wanted. But knowing you, seeing you have a different life, makes me think again. That's all." He looked around the office, and Eben wondered if a boy like Tony who seemed to be forever fiddling and fixing things would be happy in a banker's dry world. Eben looked back at his career and found it oddly lifeless and transparent. He frowned; there were highlights: good buys on the stock market, investments that had paid off well, and loans he'd made due to gut feelings that were never wrong.

"You want to study finance?" Eben's voice echoed the incredulity of his thoughts.

The boy smiled. "No. Not at all. Here's the thing; my father is not the same person who signed up for the last tour of duty. That man was tough but kind. He was a hero before he became some symbol of sacrifice to duty with his missing arm." The boy's voice had edged into sarcasm and then continued with grief, "The man he is now doesn't like me anymore, Eben. He is unkind and punishes us." The boy's face froze in shame which gave Eben a peek at the child inside the nearly grown boy.

"Has he beaten you?" Eben's chest tightened over the thought. His father had been a man who used the rod liberally and chased both of Eben's siblings far from home. That they remained gone after the old man died was a testament to the constant threat during childhood. Eben had returned to Lambertville after college, but he had never lived at the family home again. After his father's death, Lizzie had sold the old house to the town and left all of the family heirlooms to a museum trust after she distributed a few items to her three children. Eben had bought his five hundred acres on Lilac Hill and had replaced the original homestead with a house he designed. He hadn't even thought of his father or his tense childhood in years.

His eyes took a quiet inventory of Tony's face, his tense chest and clenched hands. There was no sign of physical beatings, just deep distress. Eben narrowed his eyes and examined the boy. "Has he been cruel? Has he struck any of you?" Post-traumatic stress would be the most obvious answer.

"No, Eben. He just hates the sight of me." The boy had taken such a chance by getting off the bus early and waiting to see Eben. Tony knew that he wanted Eben's help, but the answer to this problem eluded him.

Tony unwound a long breath. "No fists yet. He used the belt, but I had it coming. I spoke up about Charlie hating the greens that my dad made us. He doesn't want Claire doing for us so much anymore. So he's cooking and," there was one bright moment of mirth in Tony's eyes that showed his spirit, "it's plain awful." His smile vanished as he continued, "I suggested we divide days for cooking and might have gotten away with it, but I rolled my eyes at Davey." His face fell and reddened in the cheeks.

The boy might have expected Eben Spence to get angry or self-righteous and make some grand pronouncement about protection. Eben just sat there figuring logistics and tabulating the cost effectiveness of meddling. "Is he drinking at all?" The widening flash of Tony's eyes confirmed it.

"Late. After we're in bed. Not a lot, just to help him into sleep. He sleeps in the recliner in the living room backed up in a corner. He has terrible dreams." Tony's fingers were pressed tightly together in his lap. Eben knew this as a sign of tension and evasion from interviewing prospective borrowers.

Eben nodded soberly. "My father had bad dreams—he was treated for insomnia. I never figured it for what it probably was. I never connected it before today. My father's only comment about his time in combat was dismissive. I wonder what he lived through over there in France." His eyes fled to a window and back into a memory with a curious look screwing up his features.

Tony watched him and wondered about the piles of thoughts that never escaped the older man. He'd just thought Eben liked the silence of his big, old house, but now Tony realized that all that time alone was filled with figuring, study and memory.

Eben straightened up abruptly and picked up the phone, as he glanced at his watch. The boy deflated thinking that there was another appointment. In fact, there was a whole afternoon of appointments that Eben tossed to his assistant with a few file folders after calling the man into the office.

After sloughing off his afternoon, Eben called straight through to Brian Reynard. "Hey, Brian. I have Tony here at the bank. We're leaving the office for a little shopping trip and then coming straight home. I meant to call you earlier and forgot. Is there anything you need from town?" Tony's head snapped up, and his eyes grew wide at the easiness in Eben's voice that belied any of the boy's concerns.

Tony winced as he heard his father's voice low and deadly with some reply. Eben was nodding into the phone. "Well, Tony and I need to go to the hardware. I wouldn't know what to buy. He's putting up a few handrails for my mother. Claire has her taking a few more steps from the chair every day. Anything to help her heal, you know?"

Tony slumped forward with his hands over his face. Relief washed him. He'd been right to consider Eben one of the good guys. He hadn't figured that Eben was so manipulative, but dealing with this intelligent man created its own traps. His father was asking low, dangerous questions that hinted at suspicions.

Eben gathered a briefcase of files he would have to finish at home. Tony watched; he'd begun to notice the sacrifices both Eben and Claire had made to work their schedules around his brothers. Tony swallowed a lump over casting Eben Spence into the dandified, old bachelor category after they first met. Eben seemed taller and broader, not so gray and transparent anymore. Something about marrying Claire and loving them made him more substantial and grounded. Eben loved them in a gentle, slow-burning way that was not given to big gestures and fierce overtures. Tony had instinctively gone to Eben without thinking it through and had guessed correctly.

Tony wondered if Claire had figured out how much Eben cared for them. He thought of her bouncy walk and big grin just that morning when she bounded into the house at six with cinnamon biscuits and a hug. Oh yeah, Claire had discovered that love all right. She'd been valiant in her care of them before moving here and meeting Eben, but he'd thought she looked frail at times back then. This Claire did more in one day than the other people did in two, but she was energized with happiness.

Tony slid his eyes over Eben's careful suit and button-down collar and felt thankful he and his brothers had chosen this man and not Eddie from the hardware for her. It had been a hard decision: warm, soft Eddie who obviously adored Claire or serious Eben who was rich. Eben won the toss because he was a neighbor and lonely man who obviously wanted them despite his protesting, sour-faced desire for privacy. Charlie had been the deciding vote because Davey had idolized Eben from the start. Tony had been wrong, he admitted to himself walking next to Eben on the way to the hardware. Eben had been in love with Claire probably on contact with her; he'd have done anything to have her.

Tony smiled and set a giggling group of town girls into a swoon. He and his brothers had done fine by Claire, and she deserved this kind of happiness. Nearly as if he could read Tony's mind, Eben patted him on the back and said in a low tone, "You are growing into a good man, Tony Reynard. Don't let anyone tell you differently. Your father, mother and Claire have given you a good start. I am honored that you approached me today."

Tony nodded. He knew this, but only a man like Eben would understand how important it might be to hear it said aloud. Tony patted Eben's back and was surprised for the first time that he did not reach up but across. When he looked at Eben Spence out there in the bright afternoon sun, it was nearly on the level.

Eben squinted and decided that Tony was no longer a boy. He and Claire would discuss this tonight in bed. He blushed and thought of that discussion between whispers and kisses, hip-to-hip.

8

Brian Reynard woke alone and found that he had lost everything. While he was overseas during the first incursion of the war, his strong, proud father had died in a car wreck with Claire's mother. He hadn't even found out about their deaths until after the double funeral. Then his pretty, little wife had died less than a year after Charlie had been born. She had been his childhood sweetheart and closest friend, so the pain of that loss had resulted in a four-year reenlistment.

He loved his boys, but they reminded him of his losses. He'd been captured and imprisoned for nearly a year by the Afghan group that treated his wounds but kept him in solitary confinement. He often woke in the pitch black at the farm and thought he was back in the stinking hole with jailors stationed a few feet away. His right arm was phantom presence yet missing.

One-by-one, his loved ones had fled his proximity. Yesterday Charlie had left him on the porch with a sweet kiss and rushed out the gate to take Davey's hand and run across the twilight-tinged field. They had promised Claire to be home by nightfall and to beat the path before them with a long stick because the neighbors had seen snakes out at sunset recently. The beauty of the boys running on the beaten path between the farms hurt his eyes. Lilac Hill was ablaze with the orange of twilight casting an amber blaze on the rich green grass that Claire said Eben planted for sheep.

Brian cursed. He was trapped in an alternate universe where bankers played at sheep farming and grew experimental soybeans for the mad scientist on the other side of the mountain. Lilac Hill must be an enchanted place, he thought. He must be the one-armed ogre in the fairytale with Claire as the enchantress directing each scene.

Brian poured himself a tumbler of whiskey and scoffed, "Rye grass and sheep. Snakes! Nonsense. Those little boys are afraid of their Dad!" He tossed himself onto the couch before an unlit fireplace and saw flames that did not exist. His anger connected to the visceral pain of the phantom limb. He automatically lifted a hand to rub the nonexistent thing and spilled a bit of the whiskey. He'd been counseled about the anger that accompanied battle fatigue, depression leftover from the lengthy imprisonment, and roving anxiousness that tumbled him into nightmares.

The doctors didn't tell him his oldest son would look exactly like a boy he'd seen blown to pieces or that the sound of his youngest son's voice heard complaining from another room would echo his dead wife's plaintive tones before her death. The only child he could tolerate was Davey, but the solemn twelve-year-old saw all of Brian's defects and rejected friendship with his old man over solidarity with his brothers. Brian understood it intellectually, but when he felt rage take him over, he simply wanted to get the boy's attention with some harsh punishment.

So saintly Claire and her stick-straight husband had taken the boys back to Eben's home for their own protection. Who needed Social Services when fate and death give you a saint for a little sister? Brian wanted to strangle her.

He sipped at the tumbler of whiskey and glared into the dark fireplace. He had wanted to be alone, and he had gotten his wish. He admitted only to himself that he volunteered for the last tour thinking of suicide and the hefty payment that would come to Claire if he died in combat. The authorities were thankful that she was reticent about the money. She had simply put it in a trust. The government wanted it back, and she was preparing to transfer the funds.

Brian had yelled at all of them the day Tony left that they should keep the money because Brian Reynard was lost for all time. He should have died in the stinking hole he'd been kept in by the Afghan rebels. For all the understanding and welcome he'd received during the homecoming, he should have stayed dead.

There was a step behind him, and he whirled throwing the glass with the whiskey at the intruder. Claire ducked but the glass struck her shoulder hard, making her stagger backward. "Christ, Brian. I just came over to talk to you." She rubbed her shoulder heedless of the dripping amber liquid splashed on her clothes. Her mouth had a grim tension that pressed the syllables out of her throat.

"Get out. No more talking." He kicked over the coffee table and sent it shattering into the fireplace. The violence woke him up a little bit, but he was into a mean streak. "Go run back to your sugar daddy. Run back to your bank roll and show him a good time for putting up with all of you."

Claire shook her head like a bull ready to charge. Her eyes glinted dangerously, but Brian was too stupid with drink and depression to notice. She picked up his dress tie that had been draped over the banister since a meeting with his commanding officer a week ago. The house was slowly falling into ruinous disorder. She twisted the tie in either hand like she was stroking it for comfort. Brian was a man trained for hand-to-hand combat, but he hadn't figured her for a threat. Claire was the spoiled, youngest child who had reluctantly become independent as an adult.

Brian made his last mistake; he looked at Claire like some lewd stranger might then he turned his back to her and hurled his last volley before leaving her to find another glass and more whiskey, "I bet you're really something in bed. Eben hit the jackpot with you. According to the locals, you managed to land the guy everybody in town figured for gay." Later Brian would remember her growl as she launched herself in his direction. He tried to deflect her, but the tie was around his neck and choking him into unconsciousness as her leg came around and tripped him into smashing against the doorway. That blow sent him to the hospital with a concussion.

Eben's sober story to the paramedics explained that Brian's tie hooked on an exposed nail and created the horrible burn around his throat. Brian tried to tell the nurses and the attending physicians that Claire had attacked him. They simply tightened the restraints that kept him from tumbling out of the bed. Claire hadn't come near him in the hospital.

Tony spoke to his father for a long while, called in his brothers from the waiting room and watched as Brian Reynard signed to admit himself into an alcohol treatment program and additional counseling for post-traumatic syndrome. He received one note from Claire about a month after he'd been admitted.

Brian,
Get well for your children. For the record, I am that good. And Eben Spence loves me. He is more of a man than you will ever be. Your Daddy would be angry enough to kick your butt if he were alive. I will never allow the boys near you again, if you don't accept help. That is a promise.

Brian shook his head at the note. Claire was capable of cutting with more than her knives.

By the time Brian Reynard tried to return home again, Claire had her catering business started with Tony working preparation and delivery. Davey was training to become a prep chef with Mike Gleason as Claire's partner.

Eben watched their activities with a jaundiced eye because Claire would not allow him to invest in her catering business. She reminded him many times that he had turned down her first request for a business loan. When they discussed money, she often flounced away in a huff and had to be coaxed back into friendliness later. Eben sometimes introduced finances just to get a rise out of her and make it more interesting that evening.

When Brian returned to the farm, he found a new family living at the Reynard place. The man of the family looked as though he'd just come off of a long weekend of partying. A small child played on the deep front porch with crayons. Brian frowned at losing the right to squat at his sister's place and drove over to the Spence farm. He stood on the porch discussing his quandary with the boys and Eben, while Claire and Lizzie prepared dinner.

Tony filled him in about the family staying at Claire's house. "They've fallen on hard times. Mrs. Stilton is waitressing for Mr. Gleason, and Mr. Stilton takes odd jobs. He lost a good one in Charleston a few months ago." He squinted down at his father who had been gossiped about in the same way.

Davey smirked. "Their little girl is kind of funny." He rolled his eyes when Tony glared at him.

Charlie added, "I like her. She can name any bird or animal and tell their Latin names. She's good at fishing and hiking." He grinned at Tony because they had tested the little girl and looked up the names she gave for the common deer, the blue jays and the chirpy bob-whites. She had a perfect record so far.

Tony was now seventeen and more confident because he was working for the catering business and the Lamberts. In a few months, he would finish high school. "Somebody had to live there. The place was falling apart with no one there. It's Claire's house anyway; she didn't use any of the money the government sent when she bought it." His chin lifted in subtle defiance.

Brian nodded and scuffed at the front steps. "I've seen the bank statements. We owe her. She took good care of all of you." He often thought of that last terrible conversation with Claire and shrank from it. He might have hurt her, but the whole episode was hazy with alcohol and anger. He figured he had bruised her little girl ego. "May I speak to her?"

Eben shrugged, but Tony and Davey stepped forward. Charlie spoke up before they could bar the way. "Daddy, you were mean to her. You hurt her and made her cry for weeks. We couldn't do anything for her." Even at eight, Charlie knew it was too soon. He was the only one who knew Claire might be having another baby like she'd lost the night his father went to the hospital. "Please leave her alone right now." Charlie's childish wisdom sobered all of them.

Eben's throat filled with grief because she hadn't told him about the miscarriage until Brian was safely out of their reach. He had raged in a quiet urge to silence that had finally been pierced when he woke a week later and realized he'd been living like an automaton. He was an old man, he reasoned. He had been a confirmed bachelor who was insulated from experiences like the loss of a child. And then he'd met Claire Reynard.

He'd rolled over the moment he woke to the emptiness and found her sitting on the porch in the dark. He had pulled a sobbing Claire into the hollow of his body. He had refused to let her go. He broke her out of her secluded grief by insisting on caresses and whispers of love.

Now looking at the man who mashed down their first happiness and forced them to rebuild it from ashes, Eben was torn with the desire to keep peace but also to rend and tear. "Give it time, Brian. Let's see if you're allowed in the house for dinner."

Brian gave a bit of a bitter laugh and sneered, "Nice to know to you get a vote." He was going through his mental catalog of friends nearby who might take him in if he couldn't stay with the Spence family.

Eben pivoted on his heel, "If I didn't love your boys, Brian, you would never see Claire again." Eben Spence was a cold, serious man who did not have time for charity, especially toward self-destructive men. His first gut dislike of Brian Reynard had been correct.

Claire's voice was sharp and made them all jump as she appeared in the doorway, "I take it you want dinner. You can sleep here tonight as long as you don't raise your voice, insult any of us or drink. Understand?"

Brian nodded and moved forward to embrace her as he had each of the boys. She evaded his touch. Her voice was anguished, "Let's take our time." Brian Reynard found himself at the table with his family that night, but he had lost the feeling of being tucked in its bosom. He sat in Eben Spence's house and found he was a very lonely man.

A Lilac Hill Story 2

The Truth According to Maples

1

The yellow and brighter orange splash of leaves just turning from summer green absorb the light best just after sunset. Bare light from a sky darkening beyond the enclosure of trees is captured by the brighter hues and is swallowed by the great pines, now some color between deep green and black. If you look up to the pines in this light, every brushy arm of needles is sketched against the grey palate of fading light. Headlights from the scattered traffic, now measurably slower except the boy from the corner house with a new license and a battered Jeep, pass and sometimes flick on high beams. They don't have dogs to rush home to and walk before the pitch dark. These are walks to wear a body out before bed. In autumn, walking in the fading light with the dog as an excuse is the only way to absorb a bit of natural light. The shut-in months are upon us and make us nothing more than silhouettes smudged on the frosted glass of our hothouse existence.

The desire to cosset and protect the fledglings of the dovecote produce the most spoiled progeny. My nest had been densely feathered, but the fall from safety when adulthood became inescapable was harsh and sudden. I often walked the dog through the small town that had become my new haven, stared at the trees in the fading light, and dreamed about comfort that might have trotted just a few steps before me, just out of reach.

The dog, a large shambling mutt my friend gave me for protection, sniffed out every rabbit trail, the traces of other dogs marking their spots, and any frail scent of edible matter. When the big animal skittered back at a distant backfire or the bark of another creature, I chuckled quietly. This animal was thin protection for a single woman who had not been on her own for long.

After a few months of living in Lambertville, I became aware of my senses returning again one by one. The upset and depression that came from up-ending my life had dulled my system for anything but adrenaline-laced survival during my escape from Boston. I witnessed the colors changing at twilight for months before I squinted and actually saw them.

After insensate months, but before the air turned warm, I noticed that the dog's ruff was coarser than her silky, blond ears when I fondled them to keep her still before we crossed the last, few streets before home. I would feed her and sit at the small table in my apartment and watch her eat. Later I would realize that I had stopped eating except to quiet my stomach because I hadn't tasted anything in months.

Self-protection had become a way of life since I stumbled from the parental nest and fell flat on my face. My generous friend Sarah Monroe might have looked at my clothes, my smart little car and remembered the plush apartment I once shared with her back in Boston. She might have figured that I had it made.

Sarah had packed her bags and left the city the same year I discovered the thin meanness of my perfect existence. I walked across the stage the same day she missed commencement and accepted my degree to the applause of my family. Sarah had been starting her life over in this little town while I was blithely agreeing to ruin mine. After the dinner party to celebrate the conferring of my degree, a whole landslide of missteps began and eventually threw me far away from safety. That summer, I accepted a ring and a promise from a man my parents gushed over and began a new bachelor's degree in "lies loved ones tell you." It took me one year of expert manipulation by family and fiancée, but I eventually noticed I'd been fooled.

Months of gnashing teeth and nightmares elapsed before I followed the directions scribbled onto the back of an invitation for the Thanksgiving dinner that I imagine she sent as a token two years ago when we were friends. I think, at the time, she missed Boston and the comfort of ready friends, dependable public transportation and shops on every corner. In Boston, there were no children to tend, storms to weather or struggles just to garner basic supplies. When I first saw the little town nestled between the mountains a few winding turns off the main road through West Virginia, my heart fell with dismay for her.

Only two years later, I walked Lambertville every evening with my borrowed dog and tried not to let myself call Boston and return to my accustomed nest of false comfort. I perched on a precipice between returning to a known evil and starving in the peace of freedom. I understood pain and walked forward into the gut-wrenching unknown. At least I had the dog for company.

2

All my senses returned in unfortunate clarity the day I interviewed at Lilac Hill Research. My prospective boss, Jason Lambert, repulsed me on contact. Sarah met me at the car when I pulled up next to her old import the first day she lured me to the Lambert Mansion. She'd been fidgety, but that was normal for her. She was covered by a stained apron that wrapped from her neck to knees and nearly across her backside as if her kitchen-wear had been designed for a giant. Sarah was no small person—probably 5'10" and square-shouldered with slightly more defined muscles than the student and chef I remembered from Boston.

Sarah had originally lured me to Lilac Hill during her first year living there for a convivial Thanksgiving dinner with a side of handsome, disposable man, namely Walt Stone. I discovered quickly that the touted man was neither an appetizer, first course nor any other entrée.

And was he a keeper. Walt was all dark hair and eyes, a long, fit frame, and better, he appeared intelligent and gentle in demeanor. Walt also owned his own liquor distributorship; that's West Virginia slang for loaded. All of Sarah's friends and relatives quickly understood, though she didn't, that the man had chosen her. There would be no one else distracting him for the duration.

That duration stretched into one long purgatory for Walt because it was extended by Sarah's reticence. I knew her well; she could outlast the attentions of most men, so I felt sorry for Walt and the other men who crowded her and lavished their attention in response to her waif-like play-acting. My Boston friends and I flirted with the men she introduced and met the staff of the big mansion where she worked. We had a wonderful holiday in the country and then fled back to our studies, jobs and regular boyfriends.

Lambertville had interested me more than the rest of the guests. The slower pace lured me into a tour of the white clapboard church with the tall spire, a sober, stone-faced bank like a fortress right in the middle of town, and the charming mix of tavern, furniture store, public library and old-time barber shop across from a busy hardware and lumberyard. The grocery, once a Piggly-Wiggly back in the day, started the main street which ended with a sweet diner that was three sides of huge, glass windows.

In the evening when I walked the dog at twilight, the diner customers in the booths and seated at the ice cream bar looked like an Edward Hopper painting. The owner was the main chef and looked the part with a white apron covering a big belly; he also wore a battered, old-time straw fedora with a red and black striped ribbon around the crown. The usual waitress wore her curly, red hair in a high ponytail and favored jeans over the expected blue and white uniform that the daytime staff wore. The picture they made talking with customers cheered me when I was most alone during the first few months.

The town eased out to little neighborhoods of varying style: one newer section was shaped like a pocket from the 1970s with cabin-like multi-levels; another was a post-war grid of tidy brick and mortar cottages; a few larger homes were tucked into shady lawns with spreading trees; and as a side note like a spur, a small dilapidated area with old houses were cut into multiple apartments. On the outskirts of town, a few apartment complexes crouched like low brick boxes and housed the newer residents drawn by jobs at the mine, the quarry, a shoe factory and a few other large employers spread over a forty mile swath cut by the highway through the winding valley.

When I moved to Lambertville during the early spring that followed the evisceration of my former life, I found a small apartment on the second floor of a house in that little fringe of the spur-like neighborhood. The first floor was inhabited by a noisy family with two cats and an old hound dog. The teenage boy sometimes played his thumping music a little loudly, and the smell of fried food sometimes engulfed the stairwell, but the resident noisiness of their lives kept me from total isolation. I often visited Sarah and Walt at their home on Lilac Hill, walked the town twice a day and decided to get a job instead of coasting like I had been doing in Boston.

Walking the dog Sarah gave me in a fit of concern and affection, I felt myself settling into a motion that I hoped was slightly forward instead of the stasis that had captured me at home in the cold north. I imagined myself back to the girl who visited that first November who'd been bold, shiny and new. I still looked like her, but inside I was overturned, cracked and slowly falling to pieces. After I met Jason Lambert for the first time, I understood that I had been deceiving myself about slipping back into that happy, unaffected girl again.

She was gone; Georgiana Ensky was a new, fractured person who walked in that other girl's place.

The old Georgiana Ensky would never have sneered at a man like Jason Lambert. My old self would have been respectful and just a bit awed by the beautiful mansion, the good antiques and museum-quality artwork in every room. My eyes had widened at the evidence of wealth that even the tapestry-like gold and blue drapes in the large, formal sitting room revealed. Sarah had deposited me in the lavish room to wait for my luncheon appointment with the president of the firm. This first meeting would double as an employment interview.

I saw my reflection in the dark glass of a bookcase a few feet from my perch on a couch facing a dainty table set with a tea service, plates of cake, sandwiches and fruit. The woman in the glass frowned at me and hunched her shoulders as she tugged her skirt to a reasonable length. And then he arrived.

The air that Jason Lambert brought into the room with him was dank and slightly moldy. Sarah had told me that the research company dealt with government contracts and that Lambert specialized in biology. She'd said nothing about mold or dust—she left that out entirely. My nose twitched trying to ferret out the source of the base note that made my eyes water. I was reminded of the cloying odor of myrrh in churches during the funerals or Lenten services. I shivered and rocked the china with my knees which made him frown.

I regretted, after months had elapsed, the moment I looked up and stood to greet him; my face was probably screwed into that moment you squash the urge to say, "Phew! What a smell!" like a child. I was extending my hand for his to shake and quickly dropped it back to my side. Jason Lambert might have been wearing a Halloween mask with silver lines of repaired scars tunneling over half of his face and melting into burn scars across his cheek, down his neck into his lab coat collar then stretching over one misshapen ear and into lava-like skin where hair once grew. He was holding a sheet of paper in one hand and a tablet computer in the other. I blinked with mouth open because his eyes boldly flashed over me—top to bottom.

"Close your mouth, Miss Ensky. I expected something different, also. How well do you know Sarah?" He might have been wavering between staying to torture me and walking out to chase Sarah down for an interrogation. I could see his irritation boiling into anger.

At that moment, the new person I'd become in the months since I last walked Lambertville emerged from her painful cocoon. I shut my mouth, plopped myself back onto the couch and poured two cups from the silver pot at the center of the service and gestured at him like I was a duchess to sit. The slight growl that escaped his throat made me wince. The scent of coffee covered the dusky odor of incense for a moment and allowed me to grimace into a smile. "At least have your coffee and some of this meal Sarah prepared before you run back to whatever," again my nostrils quivered, "poisonous spore you're developing that smells like something out of an ancient ruin."

He sat down after a huffed laugh and took the cup and saucer with the same tremble in his hands that wracked mine. We looked like accident victims palsied by shock. He wore his scars on the outside, and mine ate me from within. He repeated his request with a censorious snarl, "You'd hardly travel in the same social circles back in Boston. How did you originally meet Sarah Monroe?" As I passed him the milk and sugar, I noted his preferences out of long habit with strangers I might need to please. The urge to soothe him was automatic and nauseating when I caught myself wanting to excuse his rude behavior.

He took a half sandwich, and so did I. I watched his mouth open and close over one corner and then I spoke, "Sarah and I met in an art class. I was the professor's assistant, and she was finishing prerequisites. Everything she drew or painted related to food or a picturesque farm with a lovely mountain in the background. Her restaurant catered one of our faculty events and then a party at my home . . . my parents' home . . ." My throat closed up thinking about the engagement party I'd organized at the same restaurant. I looked back up to find him distracted by the screen of the tablet. "We became friends when I took a job coordinating events at Majorane." I glanced at my reflection in the glass doors of the bookcase again; the woman in the dark glass had red hair, white arms and a stained mouth. At one time, I had been told she was very beautiful.

The scarred man allowed silence to envelop us. I took a branch of red grapes and examined their color against the plate. Rose, green and deep violet mottled their tight, damp surfaces; they would be too noisy to pop into my mouth and explode with my teeth, so I studied them instead of looking back up at him. I heard him shift in his chair and stare at my pretended reverie.

"Sarah says that you have, unbelievably, an accounting and fine arts degree." I nodded and shrugged. He was much calmer; the silence had soothed us both. He continued, "Is this a new direction in higher education? Sarah has an advanced degree in accounting. In fact like you, she is a CPA, yet she graduated from a culinary institute and cooks for us here at the mansion. You are probably friends due to some virulent eccentricity sweeping New England universities." He was trying to be urbane though he smelled like an old church, green moss and wet stone.

I let myself smile; barely letting my lips peek past confusion. "We aren't best friends, but I like her, oddness and all." I let my eyes retrace the scars, the old path that fire had left and the blue of his intense eyes. Half of his face and scalp were untouched—whole and unblemished, framed by close-cropped jet black hair. His lips and chin were perfectly angular and bent into a frown. "Sarah says your accountant embezzled from your contracts and nearly ruined you. She says that she won't have time to do your books with the new baby and her other business."

Jason Lambert agreed, "Both are growing." Then his voice dipped to sour irony, "However, I don't know if I want some spoiled debutante who's hiding from family responsibility in the hills of West Virginia to keep my books. After all this upheaval, I do not need some flighty, rich girl to leave in the middle of an audit. I might be better off with the embezzler." He'd cocked an eyebrow high which had probably cost him a bit of effort. He glanced back to the tablet. There were pictures and articles about the Ensky fortunes and foibles.

My blood boiled and fizzed; he was reviewing my résumé in one hand, and all the articles featuring my family and my fall from grace a few months ago on the other hand. The fall had broken me in a profound way invisible to the eye. Just as the twilight allowed the autumn leaves to gobble up every stray molecule of color, the pain of my fall had stolen sensation from my daily life.

Under Jason Lambert's critical perusal, the sensate world returned instantaneously. I began to pop the grapes into my mouth and slice their fragile spheres with my sharp teeth. They were cool and clean but just barely sweet. I closed my eyes to absorb the pleasure and the sharp pain of their tartness. They were the best food I'd eaten in my life. I swallowed them and glared at Jason Lambert. I lifted the teacup and took one little sip and then replaced it gently. I looked at Jason Lambert and hissed, "If you want a good accountant, Sarah knows how to contact me."

I snatched the résumé out of his hand, crumpled it up and tossed it into the trash. All my references were too far away. There was no need for the degree or the positions I'd rather not use. I would never live in my childhood home again or seek shelter with my parents. I had lived on the fringe of survival in a dulled state. Thanks to meeting Jason Lambert, I was painfully aware of my thinly-stretched patience. I stood up and smoothed my skirt before I picked up my satchel and exited the beautiful room.

I stopped in the kitchen on my way to the staff parking area. In the world where I used to live, I parked under the portico at the front of the houses, a servant drove it to some safe, unseen area while I hovered in the grand rooms where one received guests. I had been slumming at Restaurant Majorane; I admit now that I used to give most of my salary away to the bums who watched my car while I worked and slipped the tips back to the busboys or the cook staff. At the

Lambert Mansion, I didn't even know how to find the front door from the servants' entrance.

The kitchen was huge with four stations like a large restaurant and very hot. The musty smell that I realized pervaded the house from the direction of the labs was ventilated by a large fan which made talking difficult. Sarah had earphones tucked in for pie-crust rolling. I gestured to her from the doorway and mouthed, "See you!" I was a bit brittle.

She frowned and yanked the buds from her ears, "You can't even be finished with lunch! Get the job, Georgiana?" She glanced over to the other cook who was a wizened, older woman, beanpole tall and forbidding with black eyes and a thin mouth.

I shook my head and grimaced, "He's a vile man, Sarah. He told me I was a runaway society girl." I turned my heel to leave because I heard him stepping into the wood-floored hall and coming toward us.

Sarah laughed and crooned, "Oh, honey! That's just what you are! And he is vile." I shrank away as he brushed past me smelling, not of mold now, but a bit like vanilla. The difference screwed my face into a puzzle. He was carrying the tray with our abandoned lunch.

The older cook, who I'd later learn was Maggie Turner, croaked out a laugh also. "Miss Georgiana! What a fine opinion of my Jason. Sweetheart, he is the kindest man in the county." I rolled my eyes as Jason's monstrous visage broke into a tension-relieving grin and hugged the old woman though she shooed him away from her station. Before my eyes, his shape and the ravaged visage morphed into another person who was at ease with these two other women.

I blinked and saw my outlined form reflected in the stainless steel refrigerator; I was hideous and deformed. I didn't cry until I turned onto the state highway at the end of the long, dusty drive away from the Lambert Mansion.

3

A few months later, Sarah Monroe Stone met me on the return portion of my dog walk that took me past the tavern, allowed me to window shop the furniture store, glance in to happy families in the ice cream parlor and cross the street to wander mesmerized by the spinning pole of the barbershop. I had been taking a few clients from Sarah since the botched interview. We'd meet at her little office in town that she ran like an afterthought for the financially ill, or I'd drive out to see her an evening or two a week to sit at her kitchen table and discuss cases. Walt would come in and out of the house, insert a comment about the party we were discussing for personal background, ask Sarah a question, or hem and haw about calling it a night. Sarah said he was an early-to-bed person because of his route, so I kept my visits short.

The night Sarah met me and walked with the dog, there was a loud, crowded party in the tavern that seemed to involve most of the town. One of our clients had mentioned that everyone was invited to the party and that he expected to see me there. Sarah and I glanced into the place humming with voices, music and dancing. I noticed that Sarah, who was usually in jeans, khakis or Capri pants, was wearing a very pretty dress that hid her bulging abdomen. "They're celebrating a very special anniversary—the incorporation of the town in 1899. Everybody from Lilac Hill Research is there. Let's take the dog home and get you dressed up."

I nodded because it was hard to refuse the Madonna Sarah was becoming with the growing child. She glowed like a saint and seemed as serene. As we walked, Sarah voiced the thought that probably drove her out of the party and down the street with me as I passed the noisy tavern. "I spoke to Jason. I told him what I knew about your work experience and education. I told him he was acting like a child for refusing to offer you the job with only rumors and innuendo in the way. He agreed to let you take the Lilac Hill Research account if you were still willing to try. He'll hire you as his accountant after a ninety day trial period. What do you say?"

Money was becoming an object. My reserves depleted every week closer to a point of danger. For a girl who'd grown up on silk cushions, losing even the thin distance between solvency and poverty was chilling. It was easy to be proud with a full bank balance. Perhaps I could brave the upset of his scars, the ugliness of his opinion and the wretched smell of his experiments to earn a living wage. He could certainly afford it. I nodded and made Sarah beam at me.

I threw a dress from last spring over my head, but resisted stockings and stacked high heels for comfortable sandals. I pulled my ponytail out and drew a brush through tumultuous, red hair that had once been my pride. I had ignored it for months, so it reached halfway down my back. I wagged my head at the reflection and disapproved of the bright facade. One thing was for certain, I knew how to pretend to be happy when I walked beside Sarah and barged in on Lambertville's birthday party.

During the summer, the odd moldy smell, that I imagined emanating from the sepulchers of ancient mummies in the basement of the research facility, dissipated with the opening of the windows in the grand, old place. Most of the rooms weren't air conditioned, so humidity often dampened every surface. This was a pre-Antebellum house that had been wired for electricity, plumbed for upstairs baths, renovated for radiator heat and then riddled with ductwork for the newest furnace. Summers were rarely blistering hot in rural West Virginia, particularly on this airy mountainside, so the cool hush of air conditioning was an afterthought. I didn't care. The smell of rotting vegetation, the rank mustiness of mold and the suspected musky incense covering it made my stomach riot. Summer was free of the pervading stench, so I relaxed and eased into the rhythm of the job.

At first, I rarely saw Jason Lambert during the five days a week I spent pouring over the accounts for Lilac Hill Research. I argued with suppliers online and on the phone. Much of my time was spent negotiating payment of contracts and grants that government agencies would as soon forget. I also developed a friendly relationship with an IRS agent mysteriously named R. Wood through lengthy emails.

Jason Lambert should have been reluctant to trust the next shiny CPA who walked through the door. I read the report on the fraud that he had uncovered with Sarah three years ago. His accountant had left the business mired in a mess that would take a few years to right. The company was filling contracts, but the mistrust caused by the scandalous accountant had done its damage. Lilac Hill Research might round the corner and make a profit again if managed properly.

In between phone calls, balancing columns on both paper and electronic ledgers, and fielding supply questions, I relieved tension with breaks in the kitchen. I learned to make pie crust, jelly tarts and very good soup. As I learned the rhythm of the kitchen, I became Sarah's true friend. I finally discovered that I could hope a little bit in this new life after the disappointments I'd left in Boston.

Jason would occasionally come into my office, breeze though the kitchen, and appear in town with his fiancée on his arm, and it did not affect me in the least. After that first day in the kitchen when he appeared unblemished, warm and attractive, I had ceased to see the scars. I started to see him like Maggie must. I wanted him to like and admire me, though I had no true expectation of that occurrence. I did, however, expect Jason's current girlfriend to see him as attractive.

Nora Siphone was a handsome, mature-looking woman who wore earth tones and spoke in low, calm, complete sentences. I am young, only twenty-five and a cured romantic, but I noticed the measured sentences before anything else about the woman. Her words were so exact that they sliced through conversations. I noticed far too many times the way she shivered when Jason unconsciously touched her during conversation or bent to kiss her when they met or parted. Nora Siphone did not exude love or even affection.

During the night of the town party, I had been dancing

with one of Walt Stone's friends when I overheard her abrasive questions. "Let me get this straight, Jason. That girl is your cook?" She gestured toward Sarah wrapped tight in Walt's arms during a slow song. Nora sniffed in disapproval, "And that other, red-headed girl is an accountant and Sarah Stone's friend? Isn't she running from some hair-raising scandal back in Boston? What is she up to living here? Did she do something illegal?" I felt the gesture of her imperious hand as she said the words.

The cowboy who was leading me through the dance winked at me and whispered, "Vampire!" I smiled brightly up at him for being so astute. One thing I had learned from my year of awakening: everyday people were so much wiser than you initially thought they were.

My next dance partner that evening was the foreman at a Wheeling paper mill. He was the married friend of Walt's from Wheeling who'd stood up for them at Sarah and Walt's wedding two years ago. He was a nice man and a sloppy drunk. He had three little children, a sweet wife and his full attention on my cleavage though there wasn't any showing from this particular neckline. I made a mental note to avoid ever showing cleavage in the future. When his legs brushed mine, I mentally lowered all my hemlines.

Whatever Jason gave his fiancée in answer was covered up by my efforts to disentangle myself from the warming clutches of a very married man whom I knew far too well from his tax returns. I decided that night to require all future beaus to file returns with me before we even ventured off to the movies. That silliness made me grin and attract another onslaught of available and forbidden men.

4

Since the move to Lambertville, I was plagued by a dream. It broke apart every morning as I lay with heart pounding, ears alert for whispers of the last of conversations echoing through a wall of foggy thoughts. The recurring dream went something like this: I drove a small car in the dream, maybe the derelict compact Sarah drove away from Boston the May day she left. I pulled out into traffic from a gas station and crossed two lanes of traffic—the road was busy with trucks, fast dark cars and busses though the setting was a country-style, four corners intersection. I turned left despite oncoming traffic. The bright leaves falling onto the road before me were yellow and large—some kind of sugary tree for that color. Their rich color distracted me.

The road was hilly and rural with mailboxes widely interspersed, and not all of the houses were visible from the road. I was hurrying and breathless. There was a left turn I made no fewer than four times per night—always a last minute turn with an imagined destination in mind. Just after righting the wheel, I had to avoid hitting a large white rock that had tumbled from the nearest decorative wall before a driveway. The road curved and built into hilly dips and dives through the country.

Most of the time, I half-woke before the final right turn that led to a large property that was always gated and closed. There was to be a grand event held in the place, and I wanted to go inside the walls, walk the lawns and look over a hillside covered with grapevine trellises and flowers. I imagined myself standing on a stone patio overlooking the hillside. It was a place of laughter and vows, warmth, light and belonging. I was always locked out.

The dream sometimes started with a game—I think dominos with children—one in particular was my grandchild—a boy with very fair hair and eyes like mine. The dominos were large cardboard things for young children that felt clumsy in my fingers. The boy wanted to watch a television show that came on in the next few minutes. I could tell he was thinking of scrambling the playing pieces to end the game. His impatience made my heart ache; I understood the feeling of missing all life offered waiting on others. It was a selfish impulse; it was the reason I knew he was related to me.

As soon as the television was switched on, all tethers loosened that had been keeping me in the parking lot of the gas station playing dominos with the distracted boy and what seemed like a room full of people. I touched the child's hair—coarse, short and blond under my fingertips—and left him to get into my car and drive. I often left my daughter there with them. She was suddenly ten years old and was puzzled that I would leave her with strangers to rush to a meeting when I didn't know the content of the rest of my day. I began driving on that rural road in the same picturesque setting just off the highway of some huge interstate.

Once a week, I woke up crying because the daughter in my dream stared after the car and wanted to come with me. Sometimes I imagined her beside me in the passenger seat making up stories about the houses, the animals and the people who lived there. Once I saw my dog Bea, the retriever mongrel that Sarah had given me in a fit of concern over my loneliness. Bea watched me drive by her on the long stretch after the first turn. That morning I woke to the dog whimpering and nesting herself into the pillow next to mine that nobody used.

5

Jason Lambert did not even register in my periphery the morning Sarah attempted to teach me how to make tart pastry from scratch. Pillows of flour swallowed the slightly greasy dough that she handled like an injured bird. Sometimes as she tasted, pinched and pressed at it, she murmured or moved her lips as if making pastry was partly incantation.

Her abdomen strained against the apron like a hidden cantaloupe right under her breasts far higher than I realized a woman's body harbored a child. I unconsciously touched my flat midriff when the hidden child poked a foot, a hand or an elbow against the curve of the mound closest to me. That morning, Sarah stopped her ministrations with the dough and took a giant step back from the counter. She cast a hand across the spot on her body, smiled at me, held out her hand and commanded, "Feel him." Her voice was low like she told a secret.

I reached out tentatively and allowed her to place my palm against the active movement. She sighed as the fluttery bumping ended, "You finish, Georgiana. If I touch it right now, the dough will never rise to layers."

I washed my hands and nodded after she gave me verbal directions. She walked me through rolling, cutting and forming the first few berry tarts. She stepped back and met Jason in the middle of the wide aisle between stations. He took her hand and led her out of the room.

After I baked the tarts and felt vindicated by the flaky layers though the shapes were whimsical at best, I walked down the long halls and found them. In the formal sitting room, Sarah rested with her chin tipped up and head leaning on Jason's shoulder with her eyes closed. The smile on her mouth matched the one on Jason's face as the child hidden inside her body surfaced and dove away in fluttery and then bolder movements. He tightened his arms around her and smoothed his palms over bare skin under her thin, floral blouse.

They looked like lovers. I stepped back as he spoke to her in a low voice, and her eyes opened. I thought he said, "He must be over the moon." Sarah turned her head and kissed him gently on the scarred patch of skin you'd call a cheek. Their affectionate caresses and the depth of his voice fed the hushed love pulsing in the mansion. I fled to my office to escape.

When Sarah and I met at her office in town a few days later, the moment I'd witnessed made me hesitate to speak openly. The bank president knocked at the door and walked in with a big smile for Sarah. Eben Spence was an older man whose hair was changing from light blond to a white-grey in his beard and temples first. We'd first met during my long-ago November visit when I attended a dance at town tavern and then again at the town birthday party. He was a quiet, commanding person who smiled at the customers at the bank, but rarely entered into more than polite conversation. He always met my eye and nodded gravely at me when I did my own banking. On the phone, if I called for Lilac Hill Research, he was all business.

I had danced with Eben Spence once, and the entire conversation had consisted of pleasantries, "Good evening, Miss Ensky" and the stiff, "Thank you for the dance, Georgiana" because I had invited him to use my first name. He hadn't invited me to use his given name, so he stayed the formal "Mr. Spence" even in my mind.

He was as brief as usual. "Sarah, Georgiana, good evening," he swallowed once and glanced at the calendar behind us looking for the most succinct way to begin. His eyes fell to Sarah's abdomen which was more obvious in the dress she wore to meet with clients. He touched his beard stalling before admitting, "I referred a few customers to you for a tax review," his eyes bored into Sarah. "There was a young woman in about a business loan last month." His throat closed up.

Sarah nodded and filled in for him, "You turned her down. She confided in Walt." She frowned because he didn't nod or shrug.

He nearly smiled, but it was more a grimace. "It was a sound decision for the bank." He looked away and said, "I didn't handle it well." They both nodded. Eben took a step back and gave us both a bit of a salute like he was tipping his hat. "Good night."

Sarah watched him go with a big grin growing on her face. When I growled out, "What was that all about, Sarah?" she giggled. Inside my head, I was wondering how many men she had wrapped around her finger in this town. I remembered Chef David at Restaurant Majorane and the way he'd bent over backwards to make the quaking, nervous girl she'd been at times more confident. The entire staff had observed them with barely hidden amusement.

Sarah turned and narrowed her eyes at me. "And what,

exactly, is bothering you, Georgiana? You haven't looked me in the eyes for days, and you've acted practically hostile at work." I stepped back from the irate dominance of Sarah Monroe when she was all wound up.

My thoughts exploded right out of my mouth, "How many men do you have in love with you in this town? I'd hate to see you hurt Walt." I wanted to clamp my hands right over my mouth. She looked wounded immediately.

"Georgiana, Walt will not be hurt over my friendships with anyone in this town or any other place. What are you really upset about?" The memory of the scene that had wrecked my tidy life in Boston flashed into my mind. Sarah didn't know about it—few did. I tossed it into the back of my mind so forcefully that the next terrible thought escaped, "Jason Lambert loves you. Can't you see it?"

Sarah blinked in shock at my outrage. She frowned, but then she brightened as she spoke, "Of course he does, silly. Oh honey! Are you jealous?" Then she began to smile. She nodded her head and let her shoulders relax like a fighter might after a bout. "Enough of that, let's get these files in order before one of our clients pops in unannounced." She shelved the discussion.

Just before we left that evening, she hugged me and gave me an envelope. Inside I found an invitation to an anniversary party for her sister and brother-in-law. Since they'd been reunited after an extended estrangement; they were on an endless honeymoon. Sarah told me the whole town was invited, even her sister's shift from the mine where she worked. When I attended town events alone, I was afraid it looked like I was out trolling for a man. I quietly decided that walking the dog would be the better choice.

The afternoon of the Monroe Farm anniversary party and just before I shut down the computer and locked the file cabinets in the plush accounting office at Lilac Hill Research, Jason's daughter Chloe arrived to sit on the sofa and swing her feet. Her appearance was commonplace; we'd been friends from the start over afternoon tea and informal drawing lessons. That late afternoon, she looked like a terror—all impish with some plan that wanted to tumble out of her mouth. I slid my eyes sideways and asked, "Yes, Miss Chloe?" Sometimes just a touch of prodding yields the most information.

"I'm waiting for my father. He'll be right down." Then she glanced up like liars do, and she smirked over her secret. Jason arrived in the next few minutes dressed in a suit; I noticed that Chloe wore a pretty, green dress that was all ruffles and layers. He looked at his daughter with a bit of puzzlement.

The intelligence that flashed between them was not the normal father and seven-year-old daughter type. He half-whispered, "Did you ask her?" I fiddled with a pen while they dared each other silently.

I tapped the file folder I hadn't placed in the drawer and stood to take it to him. "I'm glad you came down; the report for the third quarter is done. Want it to review before the meeting tomorrow?" With impeccable timing, my stomach gurgled its protest over working through lunch to finish the report.

Chloe smiled. "Sarah said you didn't stop for lunch. I'd be punished if I did that," she glanced from Jason to me.

Jason winked at his daughter. "Then Miss Georgiana is undoubtedly hungry now." He took the folder, glanced at it and gave it back. "I'll be down to read it in the morning. I'm sure it's in order. You are a very good accountant; I'm sure your report will satisfy the board of directors." He smiled.

I blinked over this new confidence in my work since he'd barely paid attention during our last meeting. He'd spent the entire hour staring, first out the window, then at my hair evidenced by a question about its natural color, and then at the pattern in the oriental carpet under our feet. He had been awkward over some thought that he'd never voiced. I had wondered if he wanted to fire me before my ninety-day trial period expired. He'd seem so relaxed with Maggie, Sarah and his own secretary, but then he'd stiffen up as soon as he realized I was in the room. I regretted that first morning we met too many times.

Chloe bounced up from the couch and said, "Let's go. Time's a wasting!" I giggled immediately because she's taken that expression from Billy, the older assistant chef and my favorite curmudgeon on staff who worked the afternoon shift.

Jason nodded and held out his hand. "Chloe and I would like to take you to dinner."

I replaced the file folder in the cabinet and locked it. I glanced down at my skirt and sweater set. I was hardly dressed like they were. I wondered what was going on with everyone. "Thank you for asking, but I'm hardly dressed . . ."

Jason shook his head. "Don't say no to the boss, Miss Ensky. We'll stop by your place first. We've heard you weren't coming to the anniversary party for Julie and Michael. That's just not neighborly. Sarah is your best friend in Lambertville." He pulled at one lip considering arguments. "You just can't avoid it, Georgiana. We decided today that you needed to get out a bit."

I stared at the pair of them—so resolute and trying to hide it with chiding humor. I agreed more to keep the peace than any desire to go to the party.

Jason arched the eyebrow over the scarred side of his face when I came back into the small living room of my apartment. I'd given him the address twice on the way down the mountain into town. He'd let out a low whistle as he parked in front of the house, but he'd said nothing.

I'd tossed the same dress over my head that I'd worn to dinner in Boston just last fall to tell my parents that I'd decided not to marry Mark Edwards. It was difficult not to associate the pretty, blue dress with that terrible confrontation that would lead to the rest of the rash decisions that brought me to West Virginia. I set myself up for censure every time I zipped it up. I'd been wearing it that same evening when I'd found Mark in bed with one of my friends. I entered the living room thinking about Boston.

Jason's question brought me back to earth with a thump, "Rather sparse, isn't it? Do you have a television in the bedroom?" He sat on the old, plaid couch that had come with the place. He glanced out the window I'd washed last week after a summer storm plastered bits of green leaves and bark on the screens and storm window. The curtains were new and filmy. I glanced at the round Oriental rug I'd just bought from the antique store in town. It had been a whim to add a bit of color to the dull, little room. I planned to replace the sofa or buy slipcovers next. The vase I'd filled with wildflowers and fallen twigs with leaves from the storm splashed color on the old coffee table.

"No, I don't watch television." I had the sudden urge to tear the dress off and throw the matching shoes out the window. "I just bought the rug at Stewart's Collectibles." I added that ridiculously.

Chloe said, "Grandmother says that TV rots your brain. I like the colors in the rug. Is that why you chose it? I like your flower arrangement."

I nodded and patted the dog's head as she moved toward me in a protective, soothing motion. I wondered if Bea could feel the tension in my hand because I could certainly feel it tightening my back. "Excuse me, I need to change." My eyes had filled with ridiculous tears.

Chloe ran to me before I could cross to the door and took my hand. "It's a beautiful dress, Georgie. Let's go. If you hate it, maybe someone will pour a drink on it. That's always happening in my Grandmamma's movies!"

She giggled and broke the spell. For that moment, my growing depression vanished. When had it had taken over my whole life? What a shock to come back out into the open in one split second.

The dog whined, so we took her out, and Jason paid the boy downstairs five dollars to take her to the park and back. Whenever I hazarded a look that night, Jason was either looking at me with curiosity or sympathy in his blue eyes.

6

A week later, I arrived for a visit to Monroe Farm while Sarah played with four children in a field bordered by a clay and gravel track. The riotous dodge ball game made them shriek and run like mad when the fielders dove into tall grass to retrieve the escaped ball. Sarah was supposed to be umpire, but she obviously favored the youngest of Julie's girls who wore her blond hair in a large, floppy ponytail springing out from the very top of her head. Sarah's three-year-old daughter clung to her favorite among Julie's children, the red-headed Leanne, while Robbie chided all of them to get on with the game.

A bit more reserved as she watched from the shade of the patio, Chloe Lambert looked like a small, Edwardian lady watching the savages have all the fun. She grinned at me, raised an aristocratic eyebrow and drawled, "Good morning, Miss Georgie. If you don't come here and sit with me, they'll make you play!" She was busy with the little sketchbook she carried around like some children dragged dolls or stuffed pets.

"Hello, Chloe. What is your subject today?" I let my voice lilt like hers and glanced at the page of her little book. The girl was little more than eight, but she could conduct the most adult conversations. She'd been sitting with me every afternoon for an hour right around the time Maggie served afternoon tea. Somehow I had taken over both art and deportment instruction from Jason's mother after his parents extended their vacation in New York.

Sometimes having the polish of society ways came into use, but I'd have traded it away to be able to bake like Sarah or have a man adore me like her husband Walt did. In Chloe's sketchbook, I spied a pencil drawing of Sarah with her hair loose, her long body augmented by pregnancy to sprout fuller breasts and the emerging mound of the hidden baby. Chloe had a good hand at figures and faces. She could also draw a flower like a botanist, but bees and butterflies were her passion of the season.

I glanced up to compare the model with the sketch and smiled broadly at my friend who was now more animated than I'd ever known her. Her impish daughter Megan, her sister's three, lively children, this scrappy farm, the odd cooking position at the mansion, her budding accounting firm in town and the wonderful partnership with Walt Stone had shot her full of energy. Her weird relationship with Jason Lambert made me quail; Sarah wouldn't ruin what she had for an attraction to that strangely charismatic man, would she?

"I used to wish Sarah could be my mother." Chloe had leaned over to give me this secret in a grave voice. She nodded, and so did I. They obviously loved each other. I felt the tug on my heart and thought about my dream daughter who was on the verge of adolescence like Rob, Julie's oldest—a dark-haired boy who was beginning to thin out and grow inches.

Chloe continued, "You remind me of my Grandmother Lilly. She lives in Chicago in a fancy apartment. She's a real lady like you, Georgie." She pressed one moist palm against my cheek, and I realized that I was crying. Chloe smoothed a tear from my face but ordered, "Let's take a walk. Sarah says it's good for the jitters—I think that's what you've got."

I allowed the eight-year-old dictator take my hand and lead me off toward the woods away from the field with the game and the laughing children. She grasped at the sketchbook, and I took my cell phone which was largely useless on the mountain. We waved goodbye without looking for answering attention. Chloe did not loosen her hold until we were on the wooded path that ran parallel to property line of the tilled fields but crept slowly uphill.

The path was littered with tree roots and divots that I monitored while Chloe pointed out lichen, mushrooms of all varieties and vines of all sorts. We were distracted by strange blue-gray moths for twenty minutes of pursuit, sketches and gazing on the wondrous creatures. I thought about Audubon killing, stuffing and immortalizing such creatures of the feathered type. Chloe had more of a no-kill approach that I appreciated; the blue moths were shy survivors as we hunted them from mossy landing spots to resting in groups on the grey bark of ash trees.

When we heard someone noisily climbing after us, we assumed the bored kickball players had followed us, so we waited for the hikers to appear. The other hiker turned out to be Chloe's father making as much noise as possible. "Heard you coming!" I teased Jason Lambert.

"I was scaring away the bear!" His quick rejoinder was clipped, but I wouldn't have taken it seriously if Chloe's eyes hadn't widened with that wary look some people get when listening to a tale that led down the wrong path. He shook his head at his little girl. "Time to go, Chloe. We've a date with Nora in Wheeling this evening."

Chloe is not the type to stamp a foot or fall into tantrums. The only indication of upset in her face was a trembling lower lip. Both of us swallowed at the same time and looked up at her father. His eyes were kind instead of censuring as I expected. The shadows under the trees softened the scars and made the unscathed side of his face look well-shaped; he'd have been handsome less than ten years ago. He could have been my brother in that moment. A tall, angular set of shoulders in a brown tee-shirt that day, a very ordinary, casual pair of khakis and walking boots. Chloe nearly whispered, "I'd like to stay with Georgie."

He shook his head and held out a hand. "Miss Georgiana has business with Sarah, and I'm sure." He glanced up from his daughter to meet my eye. "And plans of her own this evening."

I stumbled on a root at the same time the words rushed out of me on an ill-taken breath, "Oh, no. I don't have plans. Chloe is welcome to stay with me tonight. All I have planned is a few hours of work and a dog walk." I bit my lip and then sucked in another full breath before excusing myself, "I don't mean to interfere."

Jason nodded, and Chloe gave a little yip of joy. She held her father's hand to her cheek, rubbed it there a moment and said, "Oh, thank you!" She raced ahead of us toward the farm shouting, "Go away, bear!" It became a chant that told us where on the path she was as she scuttled down the mountain.

I caught a glimpse of Monroe Farm through the trees and gasped at how high we'd climbed chasing the blue moths. The farm looked like a painting framed in the green and brown of the forest. I stopped to look at it a moment and allowed Jason to leave me lagging behind instead of walking companionably beside or just in front of me.

He waited patiently and extended a hand, as I caught up just around the next great tree to steady my footing. "Georgiana, thank you for taking Chloe this evening. I have been imposing on Sarah and Julie too much." His fingers tightened on mine to silently beg me to look at him.

My eyes had been trained at the path to resist falling on my face; the path offered new hazards on the downhill trek. My sight rose to lock onto his facial features that were not damaged. His eyes were blue like the sky first thing in the morning with the gray of dawn burning away. A straight, proud nose led to that deep indent between nose and mouth that drew the eye to lips that thinned when he was thinking. He was puzzling out something. "I thought you'd be a chatterbox when you first came here. I thought we'd never get a word in, but you are nearly as quiet as Sarah."

I shrugged. "Nothing useful to say." But then I shook my head and admitted, "You were right about me. That was the girl I was before." We had stopped at a large tree that barely held onto its grasp of the steep hill and leaned toward the path. One day in the future, the path up the mountain would be blocked by its fallen girth.

"Before what? Before you left Boston?" His voice was low enough that I leaned toward him mesmerized between his eyes and his mouth. He had playfully kissed Sarah right on the cheek yesterday when she brought us coffee during a mid-afternoon meeting. I had thought it the sweetest thing I'd ever witnessed.

I blinked at his question as the insinuation behind it leaked fully into my awareness. I wanted to blurt out my story, so he would be sympathetic instead of caustic and suspicious, but I did not want to feel that sorry for myself. I let a little anger at making myself pitiful show and squeezed his hand then let it go. "Before my 'accident,' before the day of my great wreck. You wear some of your scars on the surface. I understand the deep ones under them. The ones you carry around in your mind." I gestured to my forehead and took a deep breath before turning back to look at the wild landscape. "Chloe is no problem. She is welcome to stay the night. I'll bring her back after church tomorrow."

The tension between us crackled. He had touched my hand; he had addressed me personally. The pain lanced into my breastbone and lodged in my throat.

"Georgie! Speak to me!" his voice rasped out a deep, harsh torment I didn't understand. He stepped into my path and plowed me down like the bear he pretended roamed the woods. His arms tugged me tightly to him and enveloped me with generous warmth. He was as breathless as I was. I found his eyes wide with curiosity and a glimmer of anger—I thought it was anger. I opened my mouth to protest and met his mouth, tongue and teeth as we connected.

It was a crazy first kiss—nothing like the warm love between he and Sarah. Not like the concern, the patient joy with his daughter. It was anger and lust and fear with little bites on my lips, my neck and through my sweater at my shoulder. If our clothing could have vaporized, we would have been instantly enmeshed against the huge, leaning tree. He was panting when we stopped; we both listened to the sound of Walt's shout to Chloe and her returning greeting. Jason and I stared at each other. He loosened his arms, but his hands grasp me by either hip. His whispered voice gasped a demanding query, "Could you love me? Could you, Georgiana?"

I shook my head. "You are involved with Nora. I spoke to her during the town party. I saw the ring you gave her. You have a date tonight in Wheeling." I blinked and found myself studying his mouth; I wanted him to kiss me again. I willed it.

He shook his head and explained, "Nora wants to give me

back the ring. She says it isn't right to keep it." He swallowed and looked pained. "I think she realized right away about my attraction to you." He also looked toward the farmhouse a good distance away and frowned. I thought about his affection for Sarah and excused his words with what I'd observed. He could not have Sarah because she'd chosen Walt. Nora and I were pale substitutes.

I shook my head. "I am keeping Chloe for the night, so you can meet your fiancée and straighten out your relationship. It does not concern me. It does not concern what just happened." I was stern and disapproving. I understood passion, and I knew it made people stupid. This poor man was nearly fifteen years older than me, but I was jaded and sure I knew the score with love.

He merely shrugged, tipped up my chin and started a fresh onslaught. I was surprised at his bold attention. He burned through every barrier I erected and left me dazed and demolished.

We descended to the farm, and he made arrangements for me to pick up a bag for Chloe from the Lambert's housekeeper before I took her back to town. I met with Sarah while the children played a game in the kitchen with the men. I do not remember one word about our clients or their assorted problems. Later I would reread my notes and wonder at the calm deceit of my steady handwriting.

Chloe skipped beside me as I walked the dog a bit later than normal. The sky was tinged a pinky-purple in thick streaks like ribbon candy. She'd taken the leash during the first part of the walk and had been tugged back and forth by the enthusiastic animal. When we crossed the street for the first time, she turned over the leash without comment and proceeded to hold onto my skirt like a small, trailing anchor. I smiled down at her as we waited for oncoming traffic. She was wearing her grandmother's jaunty scarf that swirled the burnt-orange and yellow of maple leaves which made her eyes bluer. Her eyes were rimmed with thick, black lashes.

When she tilted her face up to smile back, a bolt of

recognition rocketed through me. Was she the daughter in the dream? I tried to think what she might look like at ten or eleven; her mother must have been a beautiful woman with a thin, willow-fragile carriage because the only evidence of Jason in the child was eye color and perhaps the hint of a patrician nose like Chloe's grandmother Isabel.

I blinked as a wave of sorrow rushed into my heart because I remembered the moment I usually left the dream daughter in the gas station with strangers. I blew out a breath over my fanciful thoughts. Perhaps Sarah was right about becoming too lonely in this new life.

7

I half-expected Jason Lambert to come chasing me, but the following week brought meetings with representatives from the Pentagon for him and the IRS on my end. The interview with the Internal Revenue's R. Wood was heralded by one, brief email, "In your area. Will visit Monday afternoon between 3 and 4 p.m." I blinked a few times and ran to the kitchen to confab with Sarah about the events of the embezzling scandal four years ago. I had been untangling the mess of fake entries and debits that hid the siphoning of funds from the original company, Lambert Research. I hadn't truly investigated the whole affair. Any visit by the IRS was worrisome, and I was a first year accountant for a firm that had a tenuous hold on solvency.

Sarah's advice was sobering. "I'll sit with you during the meeting if you need me, but keep this Wood person away from the labs. Maggie says the Pentagon is sending some high-placed negotiator to talk Jason out of one of his overseas contracts. Tempers will be rising." She kneaded bread dough, as she ground out her words. I could tell that her back was aching. I made eye contact with Maggie who was glaring at my intrusion into her kitchen and nodded. I backed out of involving Sarah in any of the tribulations with the IRS.

R. Wood turned out to be a bored, forty-year-old man in a tired, black suit with short, graying hair and just a bit too much curiosity about my past. "Your parents are asking about you all over Boston." That was his opening parlay after a quick review of the taxes as we sat down for tea served by an irritated Billy who grumbled over doing the housekeeper's work. Billy cast me a look that asked if I wanted the cavalry to come to my defense. I pursed my lips and shook my head for a gentle "no" instead of the insulted refusal he might have expected. He nodded and left us to our painful exchange of information on Boston, my parents and the rumors I walked away from when I left.

After he was satisfied with what I was willing to share, we reviewed the statements from Lilac Hill books for the next quarter, and he signed off on a preliminary review of our accounts. He gave them glowing descriptions, particularly the transparent accuracy and details. He left to drive to his hotel in Wheeling without making anything but friendly gestures. Robert Wood made me feel a bit more secure in this new role of accountant and single woman. He hadn't found much to complain about, made no inappropriate moves in my direction and caused no upset at the mansion. I am a very foolish and rather naïve woman.

That evening I was too busy processing a change to three of our international contracts with a very unfriendly agent from the CIA who'd come with the Pentagon contingent. I gave my apartment keys to Sarah when she left for the day, so she could send Walt into town to feed and walk my dog. I'd snuck back into the kitchen to eat a quick bowl of soup with Billy and Lou while they prepped for the massive dinner hosted in a pacifying effort by Jason and his brother who'd rushed home to help stall the federal invasion.

Jason was baffled by their insistence on changes. "All the contracts were approved before we signed. Every project is underway—damned political snafu..." he'd left to rejoin the arguing in the conference room with a fresh pot of coffee. The federal officials didn't want any of the servants in the conference room while discussion ensued.

When I drove home that evening, it was just past ten and the lights of Lambertville looked very far away. I'd first seen them from Lilac Hill that long ago November after Sarah had come home to help her sister. After the miasma of the past day, the winking lights made the place look like a miniature designed for a train garden with the blue-black night outlining the mountains beyond the dark valley and the next steeper line of mountains to the west. The scene made my heart ache; Boston was a long way off because I loved my life in this little town. I could hold it all in my hand if I just reached out and cupped my hand against the darkness.

I fell asleep and failed to dream of driving and my lost daughter or the grandson who played the game. The dog nestled into that empty pillow beside mine and sighed.

Satisfaction was short-lived. Taking the long view, I suppose I couldn't have expected to feel complacent for any length of time; human beings just aren't built that way. If my mother and father hadn't blown a lid off my happiness first, then the meeting between a grouchy Jason Lambert and busybody Walt Stone might have squashed my bubble sooner. R. Wood confessed later that he was enchanted with me first from our email exchanges and had detoured to West Virginia on the lark of meeting me to solve the mystery of my absolute disappearance from home.

He confessed in the longest email he'd ever sent me that he had visited my parents at their Boston townhouse the next day. He'd actually presented a résumé to my father in the hopes of returning to Lambertville to court me. He turned flowery in the missive that I opened during my ten o'clock break two mornings later which caused me to scream loud enough that half the staff came running with whatever weapon they could find.

The CIA agent attached to me actually burst first through the office door with his sidearm in hand. I looked up and screamed again in an extended fit of nerves and horror, "Get the hell out of my office. And put that gun away—there's a child in the house!"

He just stood there scanning the room for an intruder, attacker or at least a mouse, snake or spider that might have made me lose my cool. His eyes narrowed as he noticed my red face, the tears and heaving chest I could hardly control. "Bad news, ma'am?"

I nodded and sank back into my desk chair. Maggie entered with a large stick, and Sarah rushed through the connecting door with her best rolling pin for pie crust. I started to tremble, but dismissed them. "I'm sorry. The surprise turned into anger too fast. Agent Denby, you'll need that gun later. I expect a minimum of two intruders by tomorrow. You may shoot them on sight and do all of us a favor." A weird gurgle of laughter escaped and died. I was shocked that hysteria erupted on the heels of anger.

Jason had arrived last in a lab coat with his hair sticking up from tearing his hands through it. He looked like he could begin shouting any moment, "And who might be invading now, Miss Ensky?"

I rolled my eyes, "My interfering parents, perhaps my fiancée—err—maybe husband and probably their lawyer." I sighed and eyed the email again.

"Your husband?" Maggie, Sarah, Jason and Agent Denby asked together in voices that only differed based on emotions that ranged from outrage to bafflement.

I nodded and turned back to the email, "Yes, evidently my parents had me married to my ex-fiancée last weekend." I swallowed. "I believe a bit of skullduggery has been going on while I've been tucked into my safe, little Lambertville life." I sighed as exhaustion with my former life crept over me. I leaned my forehead on my hands where they rested on the desktop and closed my eyes. I spoke to the carpet under my feet, "Sorry for scaring all of you. Please leave me alone."

A few minutes later, I realized that Agent Denby and Jason were standing side-by-side with my monitor turned toward them across the desk from me. Sarah was stamping up and down the hallway on her phone with, of all people,

Chef David of Restaurant Majorane in Boston. Her voice was loud with anger. "David Jennings! Why didn't you call me when I told you Georgiana was here in our last email? You said nothing when I asked you what was going on. Omission is a lie just as bold-faced as an actual one. What a mess!" she listened to his probable pleading for a moment. "Send someone out for information. Did the Enskys really host a wedding in Boston last weekend? Georgiana was here; we attended a fundraiser together. Yes, I'm sure; there were pictures taken! I have witnesses that can testify that she was here." I wanted to giggle at her calling the church bake sale a fundraiser like some big ticket dinner party.

Agent Denby stopped reading the email and all attached addresses into his lapel microphone. He stepped toward the door and caught Sarah's eye. "Ma'am, we have proof she was here in Lambertville for the last few months. Surveillance can be accessed as far back as May. Mr. Lambert was aware of our activity."

Before Sarah and I exploded, Jason raised a hand and said, "They forced me to sign off on the security with the newest contract for the Saudis. I haven't been privy to any of the reports."

The agent nodded. "They were 'need to know' only. This action by Mr. and Mrs. Ensky sounds serious. Is it an FBI matter, Miss Ensky?"

I sighed and looked out the window on the garden. "I need a walk. Don't call the FBI yet. I'll tell you what I know after I get the screaming jitters out of my system."

"What do you want to do about this Wood character? Just close the email?" Sarah had a tight look around her jaw. She was very angry, and I wasn't sure where it was focused.

I shrugged. "Print it. I'll send him some response later when I'm calmer. I really liked him; he treated me like I was capable instead of some hollow pinup girl like most men do." A few more tears dribbled out of both eyes, but the hysteria had abated.

Jason was looking at me with a shock-slackened jaw. I shook my head and said bitterly, "You of all people should understand how appearances can be deceiving."

My office was empty when I returned. Just because my life was falling into the mire of scandal, it didn't mean everyone needed to become entrenched. I opened the stupid email that unwittingly warned me of impending doom. I read it again with a bit of a shield fueled by exhaustion and rereading:

> *To Georgiana Ensky:*
>
> *Thank you for spending the day with me this week. I found you a delightful surprise though I was disposed to enjoy our meeting from our previous correspondence. It pains me to confess the next part of my interference in your life. I pray you'll forgive the next error I purported on your behalf.*
> *After our meeting, I felt it was my duty to reunite you with your parents though you made it clear you had no desire to communicate with them at this time. I flew into Boston by the next afternoon, visited their townhouse and declared myself your friend and offered them your new address and employer. I told your father that I hadn't met a more capable accountant and that I found you well and lovely, because I do. In the next unfortunate sentence, I declared my interest was romantic in nature.*
> *Your father seemed agitated from the start. That grew into anger after your new "husband" arrived and listened in amusement as I described the town and the business you were managing. I assure you, I was complimentary. The young man who said he was your husband after all revelations, laughed out loud and said, "Caught her!" to*

your father.

My poor darling, Miss Ensky, at that moment, I realized that I had betrayed you instead of helping to heal a family estrangement. After my hurried exit from your parents' home, I visited a friend who works in city government. We accessed records that showed a marriage license originally requested in March for your marriage. I have attached a copy of the record with this email. You can see that you were married to this man last Saturday. I am willing to file a fraud complaint against any parties you desire.

My heartfelt apologies for my interference with the pleasant, quiet life you have created for yourself at Lilac Hill. Please forgive me.

Robert Wood

I paced a bit after I opened the attachment that someone in my absence had opened before me. I started a little litany of "Shit! Shit! Shit!" as I crossed from my desk to the window a number of times.

Jason was there when I crossed back to the desk after about ten repetitions. He was now dressed in a nice black suit, white shirt with a rather fine tie threaded loosely under the collar. He was dressed for a fancy dinner by the looks of his newly shaven face and brushed hair. I felt like a windswept mess. I smoothed back my hair and eyed him caustically, "Do your worst, Jason. You said it the first day I came here. You wondered if you'd be better off with the embezzler for an accountant."

"Was that why you turned down my proposal? Did you sign that marriage license?" He gestured to the copy of the document on my computer screen.

I shook my head as confusion descended again. "That is a forgery. Something photo-shopped to look real." I sneered at it. I couldn't see him, as he stepped into the space between the desk and my pacing. I had frozen in place.

"How are you so sure? People usually sign them when they're requested. The filing is done after the ceremony as just a bit of paperwork." He was serious and a bit irritated. "Georgie, explain it to me. I want to help."

I smiled bitterly, "I know that document is a fake because I tore up the original at the dinner table in front of my parents and that joker they were coercing me to marry right in Majorane while Chef David watched. He and most of the staff were there because we'd worked all day to prepare the meal for my engagement dinner. We had planned a quick wedding with a huge reception in the spring. I mailed the torn document back to city hall with a notarized letter stating that no marriage record would be filed." My face had twisted into the frown as I relived every moment of my last day and night in Boston.

By the time I'd left, all tethers connecting the social butterfly I'd been bred to be were snapped and stripped away. I'd cut up all the credit cards, emptied the one bank account in my name that my father couldn't freeze and basically stole the car he'd given me for my twenty-first birthday. I left all the gowns, the fancy shoes, expensive jackets and coats, the designer jewelry and heirlooms like shrapnel from blowing my life to pieces.

"Why?" Jason's question coincided with Sarah's arrival with lunch and Agent Denby's slight knock as he entered.

I let my shoulders fall. "I knew the marriage was a version of mergers and acquisitions; I'm no dummy. I'd assumed I would work for my father, but he laughed and said he didn't need his daughter mucking up the works. I only studied accounting to fit into the company, and he laughed at my efforts. He told me to be a good girl and marry well."

I felt the blood rushing to my cheeks. I am a foolish woman, so I admitted, "At first, I rebelled and went back to work for David Jennings. My mother put on the guilt routine, so I finally met Mark Edwards and convinced myself to take him seriously. I thought I could learn to love him, but I knew he was too slick. I thought he liked me—something on which to base a relationship for a real power couple."

"The evening of our engagement dinner, I walked in on Mark giving his most passionate performance with one of my best friends in the bed we were supposed to share at his apartment. He told her that marrying me was a misery, and I was a selfish, little bitch, but my father had insisted on the marriage before he signed some business contract. I was horrified."

I gulped, "When I told my mother that evening, she laughed so hard she sloshed her drink on her dress. After she stopped laughing, she looked so miserable. My father told me to grow up. My fiancée laughed and said I was too naïve." I gulped over memories of the ensuing scene, "He told me that I'd better warm up or our bedroom would be fitted with a revolving door."

I made myself blow out a breath as Maggie arrived with Jason's brother who was also outfitted in a formal, dark suit. I hurried to finish before they left for whatever meeting had popped up while I was distracted. "I refused to marry him and tore up the license that I was supposed to hand over to the minister that day. My father proceeded to tell me that it didn't matter how many times I protested, I would marry the vile creature he'd chosen, shut my mouth and enjoy the wealth to which I was accustomed."

"I walked out while they laughed and ate the dinner I had helped prepare. I took some of my clothes, emptied the one account I could access and took my birth certificate, passport and other personal papers out of the library safe. I left just before they must have arrived home expecting me to be crying a storm in my room. They probably didn't realize I was gone until the next day, but by then I was here in Lambertville staying with Sarah on Lilac Hill. You know the rest."

"I know that you have been living in veritable poverty, and putting on a brave face for your friends." Jason shook his head. "Walt came to see me early this morning and asked why you're living like you are." He shook his head. "What are you planning to do, Georgie? Are you going to run again?"

I let my fists clench and rest on my hips, but I said nothing. I tried to picture driving away from Lambertville like a dog with its tail between its legs. I nearly giggled; there would now be a dog in the passenger seat and a real hole in my heart because Chloe and Jason, Billy and Maggie, Sarah and all her attached loved ones had filled up the emptiness inside me.

I flushed as the true meaning of the repeating dream occurred to me. Had my subconscious been warning me that I was playing a dangerous game and might lose too much if I left this time? I studied the Oriental rug at my feet while the rest of the room consumed their own thoughts.

I looked up, "I rented that place because I could afford it, Jason. I am not wearing any real or figurative hair shirt here. I like the simplicity of my life here." His judgmental attitude annoyed me. "I want to stay here. When I ran away from Boston, I knew I was running back here. I was ready to move to Lambertville and make it home."

Jason relaxed visibly. "Then we have a plan to surprise your parents using their own game." He grinned which turned his face into a macabre mask. Sometimes he seemed attractive and then he turned into a leering know-it-all and looked ugly again. I shivered. He walked right up to me and took my hand, sank to one knee and asked, "You know I want this despite the circumstances; Georgiana, please marry me last Thursday." From the doorway, Sarah and a newly-arrived Chloe began giggling.

I frowned at all of them. Even Agent Denby was smirking at me. When I scowled at him, he put up his hands. "I am officially not in the room. However, if we move fast— like the next few minutes, I can have the entire ceremony downloaded and dated correctly."

"I don't know if I want to get married." I looked down at our hands; they were oddly a good fit.

Jason squeezed my hands slightly. "I know. We can do it just to drive this fake husband away, but I want it to be permanent." His fingers brushed over the tops of my hands. He wasn't thinking it would be temporary. He leaned forward and whispered, "Say 'yes' so I can get up now, Georgie."

I stared across at Chloe who looked like an angel lit up in a pool of light from the window. She could be my daughter, the one I would never leave behind for any reason. I gulped over tears and nodded agreement.

Everyone converged on us. I was rushed into an ivory dress that fit me a bit loosely, but pinned in the back looked perfect for a formal pose in the camera lens. The entire company directed and voiced opinions about positioning for pictures. The ceremony was presided over by the very serious minister and every townsperson they could get to rush out to the mansion. Walt Stone served as Jason's best man and Sarah and Chloe walked me up the makeshift aisle in the garden. The minister gave both of us a quelling glance and whispered, "I expect a real license by next week. If it was anyone but you, Miss Georgiana, I wouldn't do this." Jason had looked between us questioning the meaning of this warning.

I shrugged. "Reverend White and I have been working on a little project together. He knows most of the real story." I'd nearly forgotten my breakdown after the disastrous interview and my bleak flailing for the month in between. I had volunteered hours with the pastor that I could have been using to canvass for jobs, and he had probed into my misery. He was a very gentle, kind man, and at that moment, he was winking at me behind the scold he threw at Jason.

Jason placed an arm around my back and squeezed gently. He repeated, "Georgiana, please talk to me." He kissed my cheek and a flash captured my silly smile as his lips pressed to my cheek with his eyes closed. It was printed, framed and placed into a wedding announcement for a fake copy of the local paper that Sarah made at my computer in the next half hour. She created a montage of pictures from the garden, ceremony and the gathered crowd to make it look like hundreds of people attended the wedding.

Walt Stone and Jason's older brother left us with plans to circulate through town with bogus versions of the local news, to spread the word about the wedding last "Thursday" evening, and to slip the marriage license into town records. Walt and a friend cleaned out my apartment and brought the dog back before dinner.

8

I was walking the confused dog past the horses in the pasture in early evening when the luxury rental car parked in the front circle where only strangers tried to enter the false doors. When I returned through the servants' entrance to rush the dog past dinner preparations, Billy whisked me right into the employee locker room, whispering, "Your parents and that man you were supposed to marry are out in the front room speaking to Jason and Sarah. Get out of those clothes. This frock came out of a vintage collection Sarah found when she moved into her cottage at Lilac Hill. It belonged to her mother. She was a looker just like you."

He rubbed his rough cheeks and shuffled his feet a moment on the verge of saying something taciturn cooks usually kept quiet. "Look, Miss Georgiana, I've been watching you both, and Jason—give him a chance, sweetie. All men aren't like your father or that turd he wanted to pass you off to in a business deal. You and Jason are quality all the way." His eyes pleaded with me.

I nodded and let him take the dog out into the hallway while I slipped the pretty, green dress over my head and zipped it most of the way up my back. It was chiffon with satin and brocade inserts to create the bodice with color on color in an olive that enhanced my light eyes and the red shade of my hair highlighted by extended time outdoors in the summer sun. I ran a hand over my hair to smooth it back into a curly twist down my back and worried over the exposed bareness of the scooped neck. I realized how much thinner I'd become in the few months since I'd left Boston.

I heard Billy shuffling impatiently in the hallway and called out, "Mr. Billy, please help me with the zipper." I continued talking to the locker in front of me as I heard him enter, "It fits perfectly, though it's a bit barer than I'd normally wear."

He zipped me up and fixed the button at the top without a word. The man sighed, and I realized it wasn't Billy, but Jason. A double strand of pearls was looped by two hands around my neck and fastened with a snap and a brush of a kiss behind my ear. I shivered as Jason chuckled, "Happy two hour anniversary, Georgiana." He turned me around with an arm about my waist and met my mouth with his. I wanted his kiss to shore up my bulkheads for the probable fight in the immediate future. I wanted him to distract me with a subplot that would take all my attention while the crisis was reaching the boiling point.

"Jason?" I rested my head on his chest after the kiss ended. I asked, "Have you ever had a dream that repeats?" There were voices, raised now, coming from the front of the house. Evidently, my parents had breached their first pretended calm and were on the offensive.

Jason squeezed me tighter and murmured, "You. Since the moment you served me tea in my own home like an empress." We were both quiet for a few more seconds. Maggie stuck her head into the locker room and harrumphed over our comforting embrace before she gestured us out of the room and up the hallway to face the confrontation.

Shock swept me as soon as I entered the cavernous front room that I hadn't been in since the first day at the mansion. First of all, the mirror at the far end of the room reflected everyone and made us look like a party instead of a tense gathering. Jason and I looked like a matched set from a play: in his dark suit, he was tall, striking with close-cut dark hair, bright blue eyes, a crisp, white shirt and green tie that complimented the olive shade of my dress, and I fit him like the girl atop a wedding cake with my dramatically-flavored hair, long, thin figure draped with the green fabric that revealed full, feminine curves.

My parents were the center of the mirrored painting

in a portrait of disassembly. My mother and father did not match at all. My father was handsome as ever in a fine suit, oddly-chosen yellow shirt and wildly patterned tie. I wanted to grin; one of his mistresses must have given him the ugly tie as a joke. My mother had dried up without my constant care and tending. When I looked into her bloodshot eyes, I realized she had been watering herself regularly. My heart dipped in dismay because she hadn't been a second thought after she laughed at me the night I broke the engagement. I clenched my fingers on Jason's arm to resist rushing to her and offering my apologies.

My father began with a volley that spoke to my first thought—they had trained me to think only of their comfort, I belatedly realized. "Georgiana, what are you trying to do? Kill your mother and father?" He stepped forward as if to take me back into his possession. Jason shifted and became larger and more protective; he'd never seemed like an imposing man to me before since we normally met face to face with a desk between us.

Sarah cleared her throat from a seated position before an elegant tea service. I blinked at her in complete surprise; in a beautiful, blue dress, with her dark hair pinned up in a smooth, sophisticated twist, we were complimentary figures. She smiled at my arched eyebrow. "Mr. and Mrs. Ensky, please have a seat for tea. Maggie will make fresh coffee if you'd prefer it. Let's discuss this . . . miscommunication."

Jason smiled his macabre grimace and nodded. He led me to a seat next to Sarah. He seated my mother next to him and divided my parents' false unity.

Grinning with barely suppressed mirth, Sarah immediately began to pour tea and pass the cups and saucers to the company regardless of their desires. The stray thought of a mad hatter's tea party made me squash a smile. My mother looked shrunken in the big chair. Beside her, looking like a puff pastry, Mark Edwards grinned at the entire party; I caught him looking at me with that leer I used to interpret as desire. He still had the fine profile, the thick blond hair, doe-like brown eyes and a powerful, gym-kept build, but he revolted me more than the smell of mold in the house. Mark was nothing but a slimy bottom-feeder.

I glanced at my father and blinked; my father and Mark were carbon copies of each other a few generations apart. Scary! This time I didn't scream, cry or whine. In fact, my voice was low and calm. "Who did you get to play the part of me last weekend?"

My father crooned, "Honey, you've been so ill. You're far too thin. When we get home to Boston, there's a doctor I'd like you to see." He leaned forward to take a cup of tea that Sarah had positioned before he spoke. I could feel her eyes boring holes into his skull from across the table. "Your mother..." he stopped speaking as Jason shifted to block his direct gaze on my face. "He's helped her tremendously since you left. Your lack of concern for your mother is galling." He sipped the tea and shook his head with his usual disapproval.

I tapped my lips with one finger for patience and showed the assembly the beautiful ring I guessed had been returned by Nora. It was a flashing, square-cut diamond with baguettes of emeralds flanking it on either side. I imagine the emeralds made my eyes very green like a garden snake escaping into tall grass. Like green willows bending during a storm.

My father's eyes widened, and Mark cleared his throat to begin their tag team attack. I shook my head and thought of the duchess routine I'd pulled on Jason that first day. Again calm, I smiled and looked up to nod at Agent Denby. I announced, "This meeting is being videotaped. I'd watch my words and my tone."

I turned toward my mother. "Momma? You are welcome to stay here with me and recover from whatever they have you taking." My mother shook her head, but I went on, "Momma? This is my one and only offer to help you. You will have to choose before leaving here today. You look too thin and worn out."

My father distracted her with his chortling laugh. "You are just pretending, Georgiana! Just like the fake wedding, this husband of yours and this big, fancy house. Your other beau, the IRS idiot, said you lived in that pitiful town we just passed. The only pretending we did was to save my company with Mark's investment. Think of your inheritance, sweetheart!"

I could tell he was burning up with anger. I wasn't his little girl anymore to coerce into obedience. Whether I had Jason to hide behind or not was immaterial. He didn't scare or overpower me anymore. He'd stopped being my daddy a long time ago, I realized.

"Are you referring to the very kind man from the IRS? His name is Robert Wood, and he will be the agent who makes the complaint against you and Mark in Boston for filing a bogus marriage license. As you sit here, he's filing the paperwork and beginning an investigation of your bookkeeping. Never," I sat forward and warned, "underestimate the IRS." I gestured toward the standing man. "The man videotaping is Agent Denby from the CIA. I believe he has been in contact with the FBI concerning fraud charges." I rolled my eyes. "I am twenty-five years old. I don't have to marry a philandering millionaire to please you or save anything. You two are businessmen; try to act like you are!"

I looked at Sarah's red cheeks and blinked at her shock; I was completely in charge. "Mrs. Stone and I handle clients who come to agreements like you need every day. Why don't you try arbitration over shares of the company—I'm sure, Daddy, you want most of the control, and Mark wants to arm wrestle you for it." I took a breath and sat back. Mark was actually smiling.

My father blustered out, "You don't have the right . . ."

Jason sat forward and glared at my stuttering father. He retorted, "You sir, have no rights at all. I'd listen to her. She's one of the best accountants I've worked with in this crazy business." He reached over to me and held out a hand which I clasped in a gesture of unity that seemed natural.

Mark Edwards broke into the moment with the grace of an elephant. Both Jason and I stared at his convivial smile and nodding head. "I wish you'd been this Georgiana when we met. You've changed, sweet girl! Between you and me, I'm relieved to get it all straightened out. You're old roommate is quite a catch. She subbed in as you last Thursday, but I'd like to make it permanent."

"Gina pretended to be me?" I was horrified. Jason rested a palm on one of my knees. It was one thing for Mark Edwards to take my maid of honor to bed just to flaunt his persuasive power over the female species, but quite another to be serious about my former best friend. The stray thought of Jason being in love with Sarah flew through my brain. Was it my fate to be second choice?

Mark blushed to the tips of his ears. "Yes. But she's also disappeared just like you did. The ceremony wearing a red wig completely freaked her out. I have a couple of detectives on her trail."

I shook my head. "Nothing like dragging them back by the hair caveman-style." My tone had lapsed into bitterness. "Mark, I have no hope for you if you follow the pattern of my dear, old Dad. He hasn't been faithful to my mother since they walked down the aisle."

My mother sputtered over a false, pride-bound stab at disagreement. She shook her head like she was clearing it and looked at my father. "You are such an ass, Bill. If I come home with you, the mistress goes and so do all her loud shirts and ties."

My father looked pole-axed. "What? Ties and shirts and a mistress? We'd better up your dosage." He tried to wink at Mark, but my former fiancée was staring at my mother with a faintly shocked look on his face.

My mother smiled at Mark and then at me. "I still think you and Georgiana would have been good together. Sadly, we've all gone in different directions. Georgiana, you're right about not going back with your father, but I think I'll fulfill a promise I made to myself when you disappeared. Bill, I'd like a divorce and nothing more from you for either myself or my daughter." My mother sat back in a sort-of triumph. I frowned at her but decided that maybe she'd needed to come this far to make such a grand proclamation.

The men in the room made grumbling noises, but Sarah and I let go a laugh that was pure joyful enjoyment. My only regret was that Chloe, her grandmother and Maggie hadn't been there to witness it. I realized I was becoming a connoisseur of little blessings like this moment of reckoning, kisses and perfect nights for dog walks. I met Jason's eye and saw him swallow a laugh.

"We will all be fine if we can just shuck off my father's grandiose ideas and think on our own." I couldn't believe I'd said it out loud. Sarah clapped her hands, Mark stood to leave, and Jason ran a soothing hand down my back to my waist and squeezed lightly in approval. I glanced over at him and grinned; it was our first real moment of nonverbal communion. It was my first moment as his true partner and wife.

A Lilac Hill Story 3

Reynard's Return

1

The long moments of misery with the phantom limb, the loss of the boys, and the guilt from his reckless treatment of Claire had made Brian Reynard a quiet, moody man. He worried the guilt until it was as smooth and bright as a bleached bone. The sounds of the boys laughing with each other ended quickly whenever he visited. He was observed through a veil of suspicion and guarded respect instead of the generous love they afforded his little sister.

And Claire! Brian spent the first two months out of the treatment center regretting that he hadn't killed himself the night he roughed her up and caused her to lose her first baby. When he'd seen her last week, the little bump under her apron had defied him to disturb her. They had once been as close as full-blooded kin, but now he was a burr worrying her comfortable existence thin.

He often considered leaving the valley where Lambertville nestled between the mountains to find a big city job with his

Marine Corps contacts. The Marines had offered him a desk job in southern Florida that was a temptation, but none of his sons wanted to leave Claire or the stability they'd each found in the shelter of her husband's protection. Through Claire this morning as he'd sipped at a coffee and read the paper, he'd gotten the first real lead on a job in West Virginia.

Claire had burst out of the back while wiping her hands on a towel and frowned at him. "You get a job yet? Work will keep you focused, Brian." She used the café where she was the part-time cook to prepare her catering ventures.

"Stop nagging!" He loved her, but when she scolded, his grouchy instincts made his neck hair rise. "You have any ideas?'

She nodded. "You're good with numbers. Didn't you take all those higher-level math classes?"

He grunted and rubbed his bristly face.

"Well, Sarah Monroe has a small accounting firm around the corner from the barber shop." She narrowed her eyes on his person. "She's having her second baby soon and will need someone to step in." Claire glared at his irritated expression.

He mulled over the idea of working for either of their crazy-ass neighbors—those Monroe girls. One sister was a bookkeeper at the mine twenty minutes down the road and the mother to a motley crew of three, energetic children. The other younger one was a real dazzler of a lady who'd landed a bachelor truck driver from Lambertville four years ago. Brian had seen the younger sister with her husband and little girl a number of times at the church that the boys attended with Claire. That pair of pretty witches had bedazzled both of their men into moving with them to the Lilac Hill Farm just over the rise from his sister's place.

Brian thought about the older sister's lush chest and full head of blond silk for just one moment. He was half-relieved not to be welcomed back at the Reynard place with a temptation like that next door. He had returned to discover that his sister had lent out the house to a needy family while he was in treatment. His last memory of the house was blotted and blurred by a haze of alcohol and anger.

"You want me to try accounting? Claire, my love, I am an experienced soldier, not some backwoods accountant." He thrust out his chest and tried to look nonchalant.

Claire had given him a quelling look and focused on his unshaven face. "Clean up before you apply. No one would hire you to do anything looking like a drunk." Her eyes glittered over meeting his eye after the cruel remark. She visibly resisted the urge to protectively touch her belly swelling with Eben's baby.

Brian wanted to throw down his mug of coffee in quick rage and curse, but he set his mouth into a tight line with his teeth clenched. No one but Claire, whom he loved slavishly, could make him so angry with himself. "I haven't been drinking. I have attended every meeting with that group you made me join." He made himself sip in a slow breath through his nostrils to control other words he wanted to hurl at her.

He understood in a soldier's cat sense that someone in a booth behind them had risen when he stiffened over anger with his bossy sister. Claire glanced at the other person and quickly shook her head to stave off interference.

He whipped around on the stool to glare at the interloper and blinked in shock. The little pixie child belonging to the diner's new waitress stood halfway between the booth and his spot at the luncheon bar. Large, green eyes widened further peering through jagged, black bangs, and her little mouth formed a perfect moon of an "O" as she examined the annoyance and tension in Brian. He nearly spun back around, but the child broke into a grin. "We have the same color eyes, Mr. Reynard." She shook a scrap of paper at him.

She shrugged after he shook his head and gripped his coffee cup harder. It would have been very simple to dismiss the child with a harsh growl. His eyes narrowed when she stepped right up to him and angled the paper to show him a color drawing of a house with a woman holding a baby on the porch and a big man with only one arm laughing with a little black-haired girl. They had vibrantly happy expressions and the same Kelly-green eyes. "My eyes are not that color." His voice came out rough but kinder than the one he used with

Claire. What was this little girl's name? He'd met her before somewhere else. Where?

The little imp giggled, "I only have broken pencils left here; that green is the only one in the box." She moved to lean on the counter right next to him, nearly touching him. Brian wanted to spring away, but he didn't want to scare her. He glanced up to Claire who was now rubbing her belly with distracted worry. He knew she'd swoop down and protect the child if he even frowned.

Brian sighed and let his tense shoulders ease in a technique he'd practiced at the treatment center. He'd just taught his oldest son this move after a fight that ended in the Tony's arrest last week. Tony was facing assault charges if the other hospitalized party pressed them. The little girl pushed back her fringy bangs and stared at his missing arm. Brian felt it suddenly there again and winced. She blushed. "Sorry I'm staring. Mama says I need to stop it."

He made himself smile, "Guess you don't know too many one-armed men?" He cocked an eyebrow and kept eye contact with her. Her eyes were the most amazing amber green shot with brown striations of leaves curled in winter. With her white skin, a sprinkle of freckles and the black, straight hair, she was truly a fairy child. Where had they met?

She tapped the picture and rested her fingertip on the house, "No, Mr. Reynard. It's not your arm. That is our family—real soon. My mama warned me that . . ." her words stopped as the door opened with a slam. She jumped back in alarm and scooted right back across the aisle to the booth littered with her drawings and the box of pencils and crayons. Brian automatically covered the picture with his hand. It fit perfectly under his palm.

"Molly, you should not be bothering customers. Stay in that booth until your mother gets back from the bank." A towering man with a grizzled overgrowth of beard stomped around the counter and poured himself a coffee. He sat down a few seats from Brian who squinted at him. Who was this stinking beast to bark at the child like that? Brian recognized the bloodshot eyes of a habitual drinker and shook his head.

It came back to him like a shot; this pair made up the family that now lived in his sister's house just a few acres away from the Spence place on Lilac Hill.

Brian had been banished from Lilac Hill for the last six months. He had tried to enter the Reynard house after catching a ride out to the house from town. Instead of welcome, Brian had found this man passed out on the porch swing, and the locks had been changed. Claire had rented the place to the family simply to pay the taxes and maintain the property. He hadn't liked the indolent loafer then and disliked him on contact again.

Claire was the one growling now. "Ray, you can't just come behind the counter like that. We're expecting the health department inspector today. Are you planning on taking Molly home with you when Gemma comes back?" The insinuation was clear, and Brian noticed the little girl making herself smaller and more inconspicuous in the booth now visible in his periphery. The man down the counter from him was rubbing his chin and shaking his head. He was jittery; Brian sensed tremors and intense irritation.

Raymond Stilton shook his head and barked, "Got a job if I can chase these cobwebs away. Can't she stay here like usual?" Brian noticed that Claire's dictatorial ways irritated most men.

Claire let her mouth soften just a touch, "You're her Daddy. It is just so boring for a six year-old to hang out in the diner all day. Can't this job wait?" It was obvious that she assumed the job involved a card game, horses or a bottle of booze.

Ray snapped, "Look, Mrs. Spence. It was kind of you to let us rent the house so cheap, but that does not give you the right to poke your nose into my business." He glanced at Molly with reddened, watery eyes. "I guess she could ride along—I have a few deliveries for the hardware store—odd jobs—you know?"

Claire rushed to take back her words, "I'm sorry to butt in. Leave her here. The boys will be along soon from their morning service project. She can hang out with them if it's okay." She glanced at Brian witnessing her humiliation. Between her time alone with the boys and this new liaison with Eben Spence, his sister had become an irritating know-it-all.

The boys burst through the door a quiet moment later with greetings for their father, "mother" Claire and the Stiltons. Tony still sported a black eye and the tape from the stitches on his cheek. Molly beamed at him. "Hey, Tony!"

"Hey, Molly!" He glanced around the diner with a gleam of intuition at the tension between Claire, Brian and Ray. Tony rested a hand on his father's good shoulder and suggested, "Old man Robertson told us the fishing is hot out at Willow Bend right now. Want to take advantage of the weather?" He read the plea as Claire glanced at the little girl listening from the booth. He turned to her and teased, "I hear you know how to fish, Molly. Want to come, too?"

The little girl giggled, "Of course! I even bait my own hooks. Don't I, Daddy?" She sobered when she looked straight at her father. He was nodding and rubbing his overgrown whiskers. She scrambled out of the booth and launched herself into his arms. "Don't go to the hardware today. Go on home and sleep off last night. Your mind is all muddy." She reached up and touched his cheek with two gentle fingers.

That made him snap; he shook her roughly even though Brian shot off the stool the moment her father's hands tightened on her little arms. His words spewed over her upraised face, "Stop it! Stop that head shrinking like your mama. Shut your mouth!"

Molly dissolved into tears from his rough handling and refusal to listen to her warning. She heard Brian growl out, "Don't you dare touch her like that!" It struck Ray in the chest that the child belonged with the big man looming over both of them; she'd be safer with this volatile menace than her own daddy.

Molly felt the pull of the will of Brian Reynard and knew she had to let her father seek his fate. "I love you, Daddy. You remember that." She looked into her father's faded, blue eyes and saw the end of the day with the hospital, the policemen and the morgue.

His quick anger broke, and Ray hugged her roughly. "Oh, honey. I love you, too. But you can't change what you see—you realize that?" They spoke in the coded language of two people linked by more than blood. He was miserable with it. "Why don't you go with Tony and have a fun day? Catch some trout for your mama."

Claire was crying and wiping her face with her apron. She looked at Tony and his brothers who were completely confused by the dynamic of the situation. "Sorry, the baby is making me weepy and grouchy. Take everyone fishing, Tony. See if you can get Eben to meet you; he's been miserable with the stocks falling all week. A day on the river sounds like heaven." It occurred to her that closing the diner and going fishing with them wasn't such a bad idea. But she had a wedding reception to cater that evening at the mansion, so fishing with the boys or wrangling around with her brother and Raymond Stilton was not on her time table.

Tony nodded and took the twenty dollars she pulled out of the apron for bait and sodas. She left them to pack a quick cooler after taking Molly's hand. "Come into the back with me to make some sandwiches for all of you. Can't have you scaring off the fish with growling bellies!"

Molly snapped out of her tears in that instant. She looked up to Brian Reynard and gave him a soft smile. He was not a likely knight with his ravaged body and hangdog look. She smiled and thought he'd make a fine man as soon as she healed him.

2

Gemma Stilton could not believe her eyes. Raymond lay there like he was sleeping on the metal surface they'd left uncovered for her to discover as she burst through the double doors of the morgue. The county police had called her to rush to the small hospital in Wetzel; her husband had been in a terrible accident and was in critical condition. Like a sleepwalker, she'd started jogging as soon as she entered the lobby and saw all the numbers and signs leading to the morgue weirdly lit like beacons.

She knew better than to ask questions; human beings were so cagey and uncomfortable about death. Passing out of this life was just another level to jump through during a soul's existence—she knew that. The foggy, vague forms of the newly dead brushed by her as she descended to the floor where they took the bodies after the reports were signed off upstairs. There he was—the body of the father of her little Molly, but not the tortured soul of Ray Stilton because it had departed long before she arrived.

She'd felt the inkling of his loss earlier in the diner when she served the old couple she knew from church. They'd told her that her husband's car was still parked at the hardware store though it had closed for the day. Gemma pictured the truck riding back down the state highway and plunging off the embankment after the driver experienced a heart attack behind the wheel. She had warned old man Evers that he looked gray around the mouth a month ago. Nothing could stop heart failure, but he could have let Ray drive.

Then it occurred to her that Ray had probably been drinking the whole day on the generosity of the customers who didn't know he couldn't stop at one beer or shot. Damn! She could not fall into the trap of another self-destructive man.

She felt her flat belly as she looked at the shell of her husband and knew there would be a baby there by the end of the year. That was how she'd wound up with Raymond Stilton in the first place. She had met him just after that curious, warm feeling in her belly like a deep yearning. She figured it was the egg sliding around in her ovary and into place waiting for ovulation that made her feel that urge toward some man. She had only denied one small soul the fruition of birth during her life, and she regretted it monthly.

Though Raymond had been a drunk and sometimes an abuser during this life, she had not wanted to stray from her marriage to give that last little soul a chance at life. She let the other man go by hiding from him, and in the process, lost her job in Charleston. She had hidden from the man she'd noticed as she typed a report. She had enjoyed that job and had made a few friends. Calling in sick every time that man had visited the office had cost her the job and put into motion some tragedy that she couldn't yet identify. The worry had frightened her into manipulating Ray into a move to Lambertville. And now he was dead. Tears choked her for a moment.

She had propelled them into the charity of Claire Reynard Spence. Gemma felt the whoosh of kismet surround her as she reached out to smooth back Ray's curly hair. She let a few more tears fall and then left him in that cold place to climb back up the stairs to the reception desk where the police were waiting to speak to her.

She made all the appropriate calls and checked on Molly's welfare. She wasn't even surprise to discover that Claire had let Tony Reynard walk her little girl home, so Molly could sleep in her own bed. Gemma swallowed over the odd vision of Tony as a grown man and her Molly as a woman resting in his arms. She spoke to the police, arranged for a funeral home to pick up the body, and worried over the clash of fate and time. It all seemed to be happening too fast.

Molly washed her face and brushed through her fine hair while watching her reflection. There had been a shadow right behind her all day. She had even caught a glimpse of it in the mirror of the sky on a calm spot while they fished off the bridge. At first she thought it could be one of her grandmothers, then she worried that the Reynard boys' mother might be haunting her, but finally she realized it was her own image all grown up. She was a pretty woman with big eyes, long hair and red lips. Molly wondered if the hint of her grown self was there for Tony to notice. He was her destiny—her heart's desire, but he had a lot of living to do before she returned home to Lilac Hill ready for him. He would love other women in a lusty, young man's way before she might catch his attention.

She settled into bed and pulled up the covers. She watched him turn off the light and brush her cheek with his fingers. She sat up and kissed his cheek. She whispered, "You can never do anything I won't forgive. I love you, Tony."

He ruffled her hair and grinned down at her. "Thank you, Molly. You're the first girl who's ever told me that. I am nothing but trouble right now, but you take your time and grow up. Maybe I'll grow up, too." His heart lurched oddly in his chest as he looked at her. When they were both older, twelve years might mean nothing. Look at Eben and Claire. Eben was in his nearly fifty, and Claire was just past thirty, yet they were happiness any way you looked at it—intellectually with all that sparring between them, physically with the wealth of spied upon kisses, and practically with the baby on its way.

Molly's voice was raspy with tears, "Don't let them wake me when my mother comes home. She will be very tired, so tell everyone to go home. Tony, my daddy is dead. Thank you for taking me fishing. You saved my life today." He had gasped when she said her father was gone. How had she heard? He pulled her into his arms and held her little body like she was a baby and covered them both with the comforter.

When Claire looked for them at eleven, she found them both asleep in Molly's bed. Gemma arrived a little bit later and asked them to go home. She needed to sleep for a few hours before driving into town to meet with the undertaker and the minister. Claire thought that Gemma was emotionless from shock. Gemma Stilton just felt older than the earth as she pondered the generations of souls wandering through the house. She wanted to close her eyes to their somnambulist wandering and forget that they surrounded her.

Gemma buried her husband, held a brief wake in the basement of the church and took off a few days from waitressing at the diner. She haunted the Reynard place and kept her little daughter close to home. When Tony or one of the other Reynard boys came with meals, a cake or a note from the Spence farm, she pulled aside the curtains and watched for the one-armed man that Molly identified as their father. Gemma did not want to lay eyes on him; she would go to great lengths not to meet him and turned brusque with the boys.

Molly had kept her flaming love for Tony Reynard to herself, but she boldly told her mother that the big, one-armed soldier was nearly ready to move back into the Reynard house and take care of them. Gemma rolled her eyes at Molly's boldness and growled, "You must have been an empress in another life. Remember two things: you are my child right now, and I don't want another man underfoot. Can't we just enjoy this time by ourselves? Your daddy left me with a few bills to pay." Sometimes Gemma just wanted to hide or run; neither impulse solved any problems, but she liked the thin control of putting off the inevitable.

3

The phone rang in the middle of the night three weeks after Raymond Stilton lost his life in a plunge off the state highway between Charleston and Lambertville. Gemma was immediately thankful to have her dream interrupted because it was the one of his last day complete with his exasperated reaction to Molly in the diner, flirting with one of the old ladies who had the hardware store deliver a few bags of pellets and singing through a slight buzz to a country station right before old man Evers broke out into a sweat and slumped over at the wheel. Gemma wiped her tears from her cheeks with the edge of the top sheet and flicked on the bedside lamp before picking up the receiver.

It was Claire, "Honey, there's trouble here, and I . . ." her voice dropped. "I need your help." It was nearly a whisper.

Gemma gurgled out agreement and threw on jeans and a sweater she'd left in the armchair in the sloppy habits she'd adopted since Ray's death. Something in the back of her mind nagged at her to straighten up and get on with life. She looked in on Molly and found her dressed and crooning to a doll of hers that some old woman had given her years ago. She had been having long talks with its porcelain blankness lately. Again Gemma thought that their bad habits had to stop soon—deep depression was right around the corner.

She and Molly ran out to the car and drove to the state road only to turn immediately right in a U that seemed silly. If not for the sound of distress in Claire's voice, they might have jogged across the moonlit fields to the Spence house. It looked like every light in the house was turned on and shadows moved behind each window on the first floor. There were a few more vehicles in the driveway: a blue truck belonging to Claire's brother, a black sedan and a beat-up little compact.

Upstairs, a tall man stared out as they approached from one window. Molly looked up and began to wave before her hand fell. She bit her lip and clutched the doll to her tighter.

Inside the house, Claire ushered Gemma into the kitchen because the living room was populated by rough, male voices arguing. She saw Eben Spence looking rumpled and old like he'd been beaten, the one-armed soldier she'd been avoiding was growling words and a tall, state policeman paced restlessly. Tony Reynard sat in a chair at the center of the commotion.

She hardly spared them a glance; trouble waited in the kitchen. The young woman sitting at the Spence's table was obviously pregnant and surrounded by a dark cloud that Gemma read as dismayed indecision. Claire gestured to the woman whom Gemma did not recognize. "Gemma Stilton, this is Sheri Lynn Roberts. Gemma, I'm sorry for waking you, but I have to ask you to take Sheri home with you. Right now. I need you to hide her for the time being—her husband and a few of his friends are looking for her. I'm sending Tony and my brother home with you—can you do that for me?"

Gemma narrowed her gaze for the truth that was covered in half-truths and lies. "I can't put Molly in any danger. You've been my friend, Claire, but I can't risk my daughter. What do you plan to do with your little ones?" Gemma looked at Sheri

Lynn again and got the impression of violence worse than any bad dream that had ever plagued her. The violence was coming back for her soon.

Claire spread her hands and explained, "Sarah Monroe will take Davey, Charlie and Molly back to Monroe Farm. Between both the Monroe girls' husbands and the protection of the Lamberts, nothing will happen to any of the children. I am also worried about Tony," Claire voice wavered, and she looked like she might crumble. Her hand smoothed over the baby that had become more apparent in the last month. Gemma noticed all the changes in her friend during the thirty second observation.

Sheri spoke up in a tear-choked voice, "He convinced me to tell the police. Tony was there one night when he hurt me. I'm afraid for the baby," she gestured to her belly and looked up to the ceiling with reddened eyes. "My husband is a horrible beast, Mrs. Stilton. He told me he'd kill me if I let it live. I took the money he gave me to have it taken care of and gave it to Mrs. Spence to hold for me. He went away, and I thought he might not come back."

When Sheri Lyn turned away, Gemma saw the swollen eye that had been protected under her hand a moment before that. She glanced at wrists that were red, bluish purple and grayed—bruises over bruises from days of abuse. "Tony stopped him from finding me and killing me today." Her voice fell to choked sobs.

Gemma saw it all in a tragic tableau; she knew what it was to meet a man, fall into infatuation and allow an abusive binding tie with that man. She understood coping with all the idiosyncratic failures and adapting until crazy felt like normal. Claire nodded as Gemma made all the connections, and her eyes widened. "Ray wouldn't have ever done this." Gemma gestured to Sheri who heard the words like a slap.

Claire straightened into the formidable woman who could raise three boys, master a curmudgeon into love, and force her brother into rehabilitation. Her voice was cold, "Raymond was a weak man capable of this, but he loved you both with all his poor heart." She released a breath, "Please take her out of here before her husband's gang of thugs arrives. Please take Tony and my brother for protection. They might not even think to look at your place." She crossed to Gemma and shook her by the shoulder to prod her into action. Gemma felt the fear that Claire hid for the baby.

"Come with us, Claire. Hide with us and protect your little girl." Claire's face broke into a huge smile. As soon as she said it, Gemma bit her lip over giving too much information away on reflex.

"I wondered when you were going to tell me what it was; Molly says you're never wrong!" She shook her head, "I can't leave Eben. He doesn't look well. The police will be in the vicinity anyway. We figure they'll try our place first." She sighed over admitting the whole plot, "We're parking Brian's truck in the back part of the barn and taking Sheri Lynn's little car to the Lambert's and hiding it behind one of the old outbuildings no one uses."

A loud voice bellowed for Claire and then Brian strode into the room causing both Sheri and Gemma to cower. "We need to move out now before we get any more visitors. My truck is tucked inside the barn and hidden the best we could in the dark. You'll have to check it out during the day. Molly is waiting to say goodnight. Sarah just got back from delivering the hatchback to Jason Lambert's place. This is a mess, Claire. The sheriff had to be convinced to go out to the Roberts' trailer and check on her husband's whereabouts. I think we should all just pack up and head to the city while the police mop it up here." He might be ready to run, but he cocked a rifle on one hip and played with the safety as he spoke.

Gemma heaved out a huge breath that she hadn't realized she'd taken and held to keep from screaming. She spoke in irritated gruffness as she released it, "Claire, have a doctor out here first thing in the morning to see Eben. It's his heart or lungs, I can't tell with all of you here. Then maybe for the man who'll be hurt. How about calling old man Anderson?" Claire looked white around the mouth, so Gemma rushed on, "Eben's pressure is super low, so don't get upset. Nothing too threatening. Sheri is the one who really needs a visit."

Gemma, Brian noticed, seemed to have an aversion to him. In fact, she wouldn't even glance at him after his first explosive series of orders. He looked for the pixyish charm her daughter exuded and found this woman too thin, too white of face and hair a sleep-mussed mass of rat-tails pulled back in a messy ponytail. When he looked again, he realized that she'd only half-dressed to rush to Claire's assistance. His eyes unwittingly fell to her chest and examined her boldly before he blushed.

In the hallway after hugging her little daughter to her and crooning some sort of warning to stay put with the Monroe family, she straightened and directed Tony who looked glassy-eyed with both relief and horror. "You need to go with Molly to the Monroe's farm. There is no way a man like Walt Stone will let anyone on the place. If Sheri's husband realizes she's at home with us, and he sees you there, too, it'll be a disaster."

Sarah nodded and tugged on Tony's sleeve, "I'd be relieved to have you there, Tony. It'd be a big help with your brothers, Molly and Julie's little ones." The willowy brunette gave him a quivery smile that told her nervousness. Her sister worked in the mine office, and some of the men that had roughed up Sheri were on her Julie's shift. Julie was sick over the accusations and barely believed them. It was hard to think that Sheri's husband was a violent man under a likeable, suave public persona. With everyone in agreement, the state policemen watched them get in their respective vehicles and drive away from the Spence place.

Brian Reynard looked around the house that had witnessed his total dissolution last spring. His eyes flew to the spot at the mantle where he figured the strain of overpowering him had caused Claire's miscarriage. He had finished that day tied up and bellowing when he stopped crying and drooling snot while they waited for the ambulance. He had instinctively reacted to Claire as if she was the enemy.

Gemma Stilton spoke up from behind him. "Try to forget that day. Claire wouldn't have carried the child to term. I wanted to tell her; I hinted that it was unlikely for her to conceive when she did." She smiled a thousand-watt look at Brian's horrified surprise.

Sheri spoke quietly as she put down her bag and shrugged off her coat, "Miss Gemma's an authority on babies." She looked around without worrying over her bruises in front of just the two of them. "This is a fine, old house!"

Brian glanced from one woman to the other. They both gave him the heebie-jeebies. "Babies?" He picked up Sheri's bag and started for the stairs.

Sheri's voice was a haunted little girl's voice—tired and breathy, "That's what Aubrey Samuels told me. She said Miss Gemma pointed to a date in her calendar when she was only a week along. She was in labor when she woke up that morning." Then her shoulders sagged and she timidly asked, "You haven't said a word about the baby." Brian figured the woman might start crying yet again.

Gemma's voice was gentle, "You will have your child. Don't make me give away all the happy endings. I only said something to Aubrey because she was considering a trip that week. Why don't you take Molly's room because it's right next to mine?" She turned back to gesture down the hall to Brian so that he chose a room on his own. She mentally wished him back to the Spence place or his own apartment in town. Having a man there would make Sheri's husband furious.

While Gemma ran a bath for Sheri, she sought a fix on the evil they feared would chase the girl to the Spence house in the person of her husband and his friends. The atmosphere swirling in the house had been overshadowed by fear and loathing because of the violence of the crime committed against the woman. Gemma couldn't fix the source of the evil. She really did not know what had happened to Sheri. Unlike the day Ray died, Gemma couldn't locate the agent of harm in this story.

People's lives arranged themselves in fairytales in her

head. They were born young princes and princesses, grew into ogres, were transformed as adults into devils, swans and swains and then dissolved into wizards, crones or dried shells with old age. Sheri's story was much like a Snow White tale of misery and confusion, visits from small men who were miners, but after a dark time she would go off to a lush world and discover the real purpose of her small life. Her child would heal her completely from the darkness of her former life.

The baby was a girl with blond fuzz that would grow mane-like, and she would be an angel. All this ran through Gemma's mind as she undressed the young woman, placed her hands on the welted bruises and touched the small mound that was only at the fourth month. She sensed a blond-haired man who had anger inhabiting his mind. She gulped over the price this man might have to pay for his crime.

When the story started to escape the girl, Gemma became overwhelmed. A keening sorrow overtook her and plunged the same hot invasion into her body as had happened to Sheri. Her husband was so hated and feared that his name was blotted from memory; his image was a blend of red anger and the darkness of cowardly evil. He had tied her hands, beaten her and raped her before he cut the straps to let her shower off the blood, sweat and fluids from her body. He had demanded dinner and then had drunkenly watched her cook it. He had told her she would lose the baby, and it made her desperate.

She'd left the moment he slumped forward next to the plate he eaten and cleaned. She'd packed a large duffle bag with everything she thought she might need and left in her battered car. She knew he'd chase her if she tried to get to Wheeling, and it was doubtful the little car would make it even that far.

She felt panicky as people looked at her as she drove through Lambertville. Her left eye was swollen shut and there was blood crusted on her neck that she tried to brush away with trembling hands. When she saw the marks on her own wrists, she yanked her loose sweater over them and forgot the blood on her face.

She'd seen Tony walking back through town and stopped to tell him she was leaving. She'd wanted to say goodbye, and she'd hadn't thanked him for standing up to her husband months ago at a party when he'd teased her that her bed was for sale. As she rolled down the window, one of her husband's friends crossed the street and stopped right in front of her car. Advancing to her door, the man had stuttered, "Sheri Lynn? What happened to you? Let me take you home, honey."

Tony had rushed around to the passenger seat and shouted, "Leave her alone!" Tony had taken her car keys at the next corner in a move that shocked her, and then he had forced her to let him drive them to the Spence place.

She said nothing as they drove the twenty minutes away from town while he called the state police on his cell. One of the boys who had teased with her husband had been the chief of police's son, and Tony had been intimidated into silence. This time the bloody bruises on Sheri had been too alarming to ignore any longer. He automatically assumed she'd been gang raped and blurted out the whole story to the responding officer.

Gemma put Sheri to bed much like she tucked Molly in on nights that the little girl ran a fever. She was gentle and soothing while hiding her alarm and fear.

When she left the door slightly ajar, she was drawn to the bedroom that used to be Tony's because it was lit up brightly. She moved down the hall oblivious to tears that tracked down her face as the tension ratcheted up her back and attacked her neck.

He sat on the unmade bed that she'd stacked with sheets and blankets before starting the bath for Sheri. He sat with his head bowed, so that he didn't quite appear to be crying. When his shoulders shook, all resistance in Gemma melted.

"Come here, Mr. Reynard," Gemma whispered and touched his leather jacket. When he turned, she peeled it back from his shoulders. She pressed her palms into his neck and then his chest to steal the pain from his body. She whispered, "Tony is safe with my daughter. She will protect him from all harm." She dragged in a shaky breath as his arm came around her back and pressed her against his chest. She could not resist the urge to tease him, "I can't remember your first name."

He had run his one hand up her back to check for the bra that he theorized was missing, found bare skin and immediately smoothed the hand down to her rear end to secure her in his grasp. He was starved for a woman.

He chuckled without humor at this turn of events. Both their faces were wet with tears over the plight of the young woman in the room down the hall. His son would probably have to leave home to weather this incident. Both he and Gemma had lost so much in the last year. His voice was rough, "Lover, Gemma. Call me your lover." His mouth met hers with a spark that caught and flamed.

He woke to a warm body pressed close to his; where they touched skin or the mattress was warm; all other surfaces, including the stump of his right arm, were uncovered and frozen. He opened his eyes to see she was examining his face as he came back to full consciousness. Both lamps in the room still lit their stark nakedness. She must have been cold also but hadn't wanted to stir him out of sleep—deep sleep with no dreams.

Finally she closed her eyes, levered herself up and dragged a thick quilt that was still folded over both of them. She shook it in a small, furious gesture that insisted the thing right itself over them. She turned so that her back was to him and settled back into his warmth. "Must be twenty below out there this morning," her voice was morning rough and just a bit worried over Brian's true nature.

Brian smiled though she couldn't see it. He shifted her closer and thought to answer her unasked question, but he refused to dabble with small talk. "Boy or girl?" He kissed her shoulder and rubbed his whiskered cheek on her white skin that felt like satin under his rough bristles. He felt her slight urge to withdraw, so he made a denying noise and kissed her neck as he pressed her closer. "Which did we just conceive?"

"You knew?" Gemma felt relieved and betrayed; she had denied herself even a glimpse of this man for weeks. She had hidden in the back of the diner when he sat at the counter and spoke to his sister.

Last week, she had crossed the street and gotten her hair cut when she saw him walk into the grocery store in front of her. She had denied him access into her mind and had forgotten his first name though his sister said it whenever she spoke of the boys. "A boy. You can only give boys. You knew?" She felt him nod and chuckle with satisfaction.

Brian sighed, "Your Molly drew me a picture a month ago. You had a baby in your arms, and we stood in front of this house together." He sat up slightly to look down at her openly shocked face, "I learned one thing overseas, Gemma. You shouldn't tempt fate, but you also can't escape it." He kissed her solemnly and wanted to melt them both together, but he heard a vehicle on the gravel drive and movement of the dog approaching the front door down in the hallway. He was out of bed in seconds with Gemma right behind him pulling on clothing.

Before they even left the room, she whispered, "Don't worry, it's the doctor. The next visitors are the ones we have to watch." A shiver ran down Brian's back and undid all the unraveling she had done with her soft body a few hours ago.

While the doctor examined Sheri, Brian made coffee and stretched at the kitchen table. That Gemma was the strangest woman he'd ever known. And she really didn't know his first name. He wondered if she had really conceived a little boy last night. Stranger things had happened; look at the situation playing out in Molly's little bedroom right now.

Sheri had started the conversation with the doctor by telling the man she had figured out the exact date of the baby's conception. She'd had a dream and just realized it was a memory. She was ecstatic after a good few hours' sleep that it couldn't be her husband's child. She whispered to Gemma, "He was someone from the mine's corporate office, tall and blond. He was at the 4th of July picnic, and it happened over Labor Day weekend."

Gemma came down while the doctor and Sheri talked alone and joined Brian at the counter. He poured her a coffee and watched how she doctored it with a bit of milk and failed to use sugar. He wondered how she took her eggs and let his mouth arch into a grin. He hadn't had a woman to study for five years. His wife had been a tiny child of a woman with chestnut brown hair like Davey and pretty blue eyes. All three of the boys had his blue-green eyes, and a swarthy French complexion like Brian's parents.

He looked at Gemma in the new light of passing dawn and found her much more beautiful than last night. She had brushed the midnight black hair out into a cloud of shiny, dark ropes that twisted into curling locks. She was taller and thinner than Claire and much more serious than even he was. Her eyes were a luminous green in the stronger light. When she looked at him, he wondered if she knew all his thoughts.

Brian crossed the little space between them and kissed her very gently. "Gemma Stilton? My name is Brian. Don't forget that. No matter what happens in the next few days, I want to come back here to you. I want us to be together." He couldn't think any clearer but felt satisfied when she held him with her hands at his waist and nodded. They both looked out the window and stood taller as a Lambertville deputy's car turned right off the state road and barreled down the gravel drive. The truck behind it had a number of men in it.

Brian swore under his breath as Gemma dialed a few quick numbers. She'd been ready for this moment from the time she woke that morning.

He pulled on his boots, a Kevlar vest and picked up the rifle that was the usual mode of animal control on the small farms in the area. He shouted up the stairs, "Hey Doc, get yourselves to an inside wall and stay down. We have company, and it doesn't look friendly."

Gemma shook her head. "This is Lambertville, West Virginia not Iraq or the big city, Brian Reynard. Let me hold them off for about ten minutes and put that thing down," she gestured to the rifle. "You keep yourself out of sight. A man like Nick is an insecure coward. He sees you, and this will get ugly."

She yelled upstairs, "Doc? You're needed next door after you talk to the men out there. I'll walk you out to your car. Sheri? You come right down here to show the local sheriff that Nick beat you. Then you go back upstairs. We are doing this thing the right way, understand?" She glared at Brian and whispered as a loud knocking started at the front door, "This has nothing to do with your arm or your abilities, understand that, Brian? You are more of a threat to us if you go off and shoot that thing right now. Got that?" She was so close he could see the rapidity of her heartbeat in her neck, but she looked calm.

He nodded while some eager male impulse made him flush with pride at having found such a strong woman completely by accident.

Deputy Chris Hanson had admired Gemma Stilton a long time before the December morning he had to come out to her house to serve papers and monitor the reuniting of Nick and Sheri Lynn Baker. When she gestured for him to back off her front porch and stand in the yard, he did it automatically. He had been the one to call her go to the hospital in Wetzel just a half hour after she served him dinner at the café in town. He'd gotten the call only two minutes down the road after taking his dinner break with his mother and father who met him at the diner whenever they could.

During dinner that night, his father had examined the waitress' face and had declared, "That Gemma Stilton looks like she came right out of one of those paintings you like so much, honey." He had squeezed Gertrude Hanson's hand as she bristled over his wandering eye. "That Celtic goddess in that story you had me read to Sally last night." His parents had been married forty years, but they were still so in love and interested in each other, it was a constant embarrassment to all of their four children.

Gemma Stilton was one long-legged, calm goddess as she stepped off her porch on the frosty December day. She stood there with her hands on her hips and a gentle smile on her lips only for Chris. When she glanced toward the other vehicle, her eyes hardened and her mouth grew slack. "Hey, Deputy Hanson. Where's the chief this morning?"

She winked at him. With an automatic movement, he reached into his vehicle, grasped the radio and spoke into it, "Martha? Find the chief. There's trouble out on Lilac Hill at the Reynard place." He felt the hair rise on the back of his neck when the doors opened on the crew cab behind him. He turned, "Guys, stay where you are."

Gemma's voice was clear in the cold air, "The deputy is welcome here, but the rest of you are not. Get off my property right now; you are trespassing."

Nick, holding a shotgun aimed at the ground for the moment, looked like something had run him over and left him for dead. His face was unshaven, eyes bloodshot and his body was stiffened from cowardly rage. "You give me back my wife, bitch. I want what's mine." He took a step forward, but one of the other men grabbed his coat sleeve and made a cautioning sound.

She knew every one of these men from the diner; they were all married or divorced and fathers except Nick. No man who was a father could look at Sheri and think she should go home with her husband.

Gemma shook her head. "I am not trading insults with you. She is not your property and is too beat up to come home and face any more of your abuse." She saw the deputy's eyes widen as he watched the front door open and the doctor emerge with Sheri dressed in her bare nightgown but wrapped in a blanket. Juliet watched the deputy remove his radio from the car and unlatch his revolver's holster. She prayed for Brian to stay hidden in the house. The sight of Sheri Lynn's blackened eye, split lips and bruised wrists and ankles convinced all of them of the violence she'd suffered.

Sheri stood silently as the doctor walked up to the deputy and spoke in a clear, quiet voice. The men standing at the truck shifted uncomfortably, "Sheri was brutally raped, she has marks on her wrists, arms and ankles from being tied up, it shows that she struggled, and she also has several contusions. Claire Spence wanted a rape kit done last night, but Sheri refused because she said it was only Nick. We are going to have to monitor her because she's bleeding and might miscarry."

He looked toward Nick, "Young man, it would be best for all of us if you and your friends went back up the road and let her stay here in peace. She does not want to press charges, if you just leave her alone. Mrs. Stilton will take care of her until she's healed. Then you two should meet and discuss a formal separation. She does not want to return to your home."

Gemma returned to the front porch as Nick started to rush toward the house but was held back by his friend Bobby Farlace. She urged, "Doctor, you're needed over at the Spence's right now. Please go!" She was close to tears. The doctor could leave only if Nick moved because Anderson's car was positioned between his truck and the deputy's cruiser.

The other men who'd come with Nick were shifting in discomfort. "Pregnant? Raped? Beat up?" Their words were heard over the scraping of boots on the gravel. Nick's best friend Bobby looked at his friend and squinted uttering, "Shit, Nick!"

The doctor nodded gravely and got into his car. One of the men ripped the keys from Nick's slackened hand and moved the truck out of the way and positioned it to leave the Reynard place. They watched the doctor's car crunch up the drive and down the next in relief. "Hope Claire and Eben are okay. We left them kind of worked up," one said to another.

Nick rushed past the deputy and stepped up on the porch to seize his opportunity. He saw Brian step into the doorway with the shotgun and cocked the one in his hands.

The deputy removed his gun as the radio crackled, "Hanson? I'm at Nick's house. We've got a dead girl here." The man's voice was rough.

Gemma watched as Nick turned a greenish-gray and teetered on the steps. "She was alive when I left." He was blinking in shock and reached out to Sheri Lynn who was starting to sway.

Sheri Lyn jumped back repulsed and dropped the blanket. The bright contrast of the bruises from his fists and the burn scars from his cigarettes seemed to leap off her frail body. The red and purple lines from the cord he'd tied her with were livid. She cried, "Who? Who died because no one would stop you? Who was she, Nick?" The evidence of the baby under the thin gown was obvious. The young woman looked both lovely and hideous to the men who'd been regaled with her attributes. It had been rumored that Nick would trade her for debts every now and then. Gemma was in front of her in the next moment, wrapping the blanket back around her shivering body.

Everyone in town knew the rumors about the teenage boys that had walked away from somebody's trailer a few weeks ago after Tony Reynard refused to touch a drugged female. The town understood the randy ways of young men; in a chauvinistic way they ignored the boys' roving desires to lure girls to fooling around a bit, but this was a church-driven community. Rumors of their antics had started to concern the town. Accusations had exploded in a huge fight at the town park the previous week which left a seventeen-year-old boy in critical condition.

The boys had stopped running the town and had splintered into factions. To the older men, Tony Reynard was dangerously heroic, but to the younger ones, he had just been a wimp that night. The temptation of the drugged woman, the isolation of the trailer on a back road and a bit of dallying with alcohol and pot had made them boastful and lusty. The sight of the unconscious woman sprawled like a doll in dirty sheets had made Tony want to vomit.

Nick rubbed his whiskers and shook his head, "Some

tramp from Wheeling. I drove there yesterday chasing you. She got into my truck for twenty bucks. Shit!" He took a step backwards and stumbled away from the shocked deputy who was lifting his gun from its holster and speaking into the radio.

Gemma held Sheri tightly and glared at Nick from only a few feet away. "You, coward! Did you drug her?" At that, the deputy stepped forward because it looked like Nick was about to throw himself at the two women.

He let his shoulders slump suddenly and turned back toward the truck in a jog. The men who had accompanied him stood limply. The band of vigilantes had deflated like balloons. The deputy shouted, "Nick! Stop! You need to come in for questioning."

Nick pulled the shotgun to his shoulder and blew a round off at Chris Hanson as he slid behind the wheel. The deputy's eyes widened in shock; he found himself flat on his back on the gravel driveway. Hanson looked up into the grey December sky as he heard the truck back crazily around in the drive, turn the corner spitting gravel, and skid toward the highway in the direction of Wheeling.

Gemma had felt the warm rush of Brian taking them off their feet and impelling them onto the floor of porch. She thrust Sheri through the front door and then rushed down the steps to Chris Hanson. One of the men who'd been with Nick knelt beside her and spoke into the radio as a shotgun fired with the immediate sound of breaking glass and the crunch of the truck hitting the fence at the end of the drive. It seemed to turn on two wheels and rushed off down the highway. "Chief, Hanson's been shot. Nick is on the state highway going north. Reynard shot out his back window. Shit! Bobby got into the truck with him."

Gemma and the man opened up the deputy's jacket and found the vest with a gaping shadow where the shot had punched him. Gemma's fingers searched and found no blood. She looked right down into his frightened, young eyes and saw the little boy hidden under the grown man. She thought of his mother Gertrude in the diner on the day Ray died teasing her husband because he'd been caught gawking at Gemma's legs.

The young deputy's chest heaved as his breath returned. A trickle of blood ran from the corner of his lips. He gulped as Brian laughed down at his sprawled form, "He's fine. He's going to have a nasty bruise and a few days of desk duty."

He locked the rifle and gave the deputy a hand up. "What'd you do, bite your lip?" Brian's eyes were bright. For a split second, he'd been afraid that Nick was going to aim for the women. He'd been too intent on taking them out of harm's way to stop Nick from shooting the hapless deputy.

The radio crackled as the man who'd rushed to help Chris Hanson took over communications. Gemma dismissed the problem of Nick and Bobby. They were dead men. She prayed that they wouldn't hurt anyone else as they shot down the highway on the path to their deaths. She tried to imagine a single vehicle accident just outside of Wheeling and worried over using her sight improperly. She did not understand which vision was a peek at the future, and which was her unadulterated will. Both frightened her at times.

4

Eben shuffled through the house trying not to disturb the women. The late night and the upset over Tony's interference with the Robert's woman had drained all of them. Tony had become a royal terror since he turned eighteen a month ago, and it worried them constantly. Perhaps enlistment with the Army wasn't such a bad plan if the boy could avoid conviction for the assault charges pending from last week's fight.

The visit from Nick Baker and his friend Bobby Farlace had been sobering an hour ago; the young man had seemed worried about his emotionally-distraught wife. He spun a story about her abusive boyfriend visiting her while he was away on mine business. He acted like he had no idea she'd been hurt and was only looking for her at Spence's because she had worked with Claire at the diner before she married him last year. Eben had fought back the thought that Nick seemed way too old to be married to a girl who looked barely out of her teens. He wondered where they'd met, and then blushed over the age difference between himself and Claire. But Claire had never seemed like a child, even after she lost the first baby and cried like one for days.

Julie Monroe Elliott had warned them that Nick Baker was a smooth talker and was rumored to be a hard drinker and a regular womanizer. His sales and service position at the mine capitalized on his easy-going charisma; she had bounced her blond curls last night and insinuated that he had tried to make moves on her during the year her husband Michael had gone missing. Eben placed a hand on his chest that was tightened with phlegm and thought about easy-going Michael Elliott as an unlikely partner for the golden girl living at Monroe Farm with her quieter sister Sarah.

He knew Sarah better than Julie through referrals to her accounting office from the bank. Eben might admit only when he was alone that Sarah's appearance in town a few years ago had started him thinking of marriage. She had been unconsciously beautiful, careful with her sister's little children, and brave enough to do anything to keep the farm solvent. Eben had expected her to visit his office that entire first year to beg an extension on their mortgage or some impossible loan. She had steadily paid their bills and never asked for assistance as she babied her ancient car, managed repairs to the farm house and finally reopened the little caretaker's cottage on the farm for her own use. Her partnership with Walt Stone, who owned a liquor distributorship that spanned the county, was a brilliant one. Walt Stone's gentle humor and active social life balanced Sarah's tendency to intellectual quiet.

Eben Spence was surprised to see the doctor on his doorstep that morning. He'd been kept awake most of the night coughing and battling cold sweats. Whiskey hadn't helped him sleep, decongestants made his heart race, and he felt intense pain when he muffled the coughing. He hadn't wanted to disturb Claire or his mother. He'd just turned forty-seven, but he felt older without good sleep for most of the week with the pesky cold that had turned into bronchitis. He let the doctor in with poor grace, asking "What's up, Anderson? Have you been to the Reynard place this morning?"

The doctor nodded. "Bad business. Deputy Hanson is over there now. That Nick showed up and is trying to talk Sheri into going home with him." Eben looked like he was ready to rush over there. "Don't worry; other deputies are on the way, and there's no way Hanson, Gemma Stilton or Brian Reynard will allow it."

He was gesturing for Eben to follow him into the kitchen like he owned the place. "We doctors and bankers need to stay out of law enforcement. We also need a straight-back chair for your examination." He placed a large hand on Eben's shoulder and pushed him down to sit at the table. "Unbutton your shirt."

Eben grouched out, "This is my house. You were bossy even when we were boys." Then a rattle of coughing seized him. The doctor waited with a wince. He warmed the stethoscope automatically and then listened to Eben's chest front and back as Claire came into the room completely dressed. She'd obviously known the doctor was coming.

Eben gazed at his young wife with a grimace; he felt outnumbered and outgunned in this situation. How had his life been overtaken by this woman? But then he saw her smile and realized that he was a lucky man. If he'd been alone like he'd been in the past, he might have died from the pneumonia the doctor theorized had clogged both his lungs.

He had relaxed in the company of his hovering wife and the doctor when he heard the shot gun blast. All three of them jumped as the gunshot reverberated one whole farm away. They gasped as another shotgun blast followed quickly. Claire started to moan. "I have to go down to the house!"

Eben shook his head and took control immediately. "The deputy's there with your brother and Gemma. Call the state police and tell them shots have been fired. That sounded like a truck," he was caught by a spasm of coughing again. "I think I'm sick, Claire." His voice told his surprise.

Claire crossed to hug her husband close and wipe the perspiration from his brow. "It will all be fine. I'll call." Claire made the phone call and was told reinforcements were nearly there. She was not to worry. She was dialing again in the next moment, spoke to someone in a low voice, and cursed quietly as she hung up. She stoically crossed to the hall closet, removed the gun she used last spring to control groundhogs that attacked her turnip bed, and slipped out the door with a shout, "I called for help at the Monroe Farm. I'm going down to check on my boys. Dr. Anderson? Try to contact Brian and tell him to get the deputy to drive through the path over the hill for the tractor. His cruiser should make it. You stay here with Eben, okay?"

She ignored Eben's hacking shout to stop. All the way up the road, Claire rewound the impulse that had forced her out of her little house in Richmond to move the boys to Lambertville two years ago. What had she been thinking? The dangers of drugs and gangs in the city were no more a threat to the boys than this provincial town that looked like a postcard on the surface. Working in the diner and listening to Eben worry over loans he approved had sobered her up.

There was evil and cowardice even in the safe little town, but here it seemed more insidious because she knew these people—no one was truly pure evil or good. You knew all the little histories of nobility, flaws and just ordinary tragedy that made people what they were. It was hard to blame them for acting out their little dramas like they did, but everyone in a small town watched, commented, grieved and rejoiced. The broken girl that she had foisted on Gemma Stilton last night was a casebook tragedy.

She corrected herself when she saw Sarah Monroe standing out in the drive beside Tony as he faced a gang of boys. These boys were the ones who had driven onto their property to "speak" with Tony Reynard before the big fight in the town park last weekend. Claire marveled at the young woman—that Sarah was good all the way through and strong like a fiery, guardian angel. Her long, brown hair whipped around her body with the cold morning breezes as she spoke to them. She was giving a stern lecture to the gathering as Tony stood impassively quiet but holding her hand. Behind them on the porch, Sarah's husband Walt, her sister Julie and husband Michael listened. The children waited behind the closed screen door though it was bitter December. No one brandished a weapon.

A few of the boys began to retreat when Claire pulled up next to Sarah's little import. The arrival of Mrs. Reynard-Spence was like being caught by your mother. Most of these boys had been out to the Reynard or Spence place for the parties she still threw for every birthday as if the boys were perpetually turning five. Everyone liked old Eben Spence's young wife whether it was from her role as mother to the Reynard boys or the cook at the diner in town. And Mr. Spence ran Lambertville's bank—there was no need to make enemies here.

Some were relieved the night Tony called them all despicable for even thinking about touching the woman who slept inert and splayed on her bed. But he had shamed them and yelled about it all the way home in a pent-up burst of frustrated lust and angered them. He'd railed on like a preacher—of course that woman was beautiful and available, but she was completely defenseless. What was wrong with them? They'd have to see that woman on the streets of Lambertville and attend church with her.

They been quiet during his tirade but slowly started to giggle at themselves and then began to berate him. "Coward" and "pussy" had been the chorus by the time they reached the safety of the Lambertville Town Park.

Then he made them all angry with him when he failed to back down and cruelly suggested, "Hey, Sam. Why don't we get your little sister drunk and do the same to her? You all make me sick." The guys who had taken their turn touching Sheri felt sick once the high they were on diminished. It was the end of friendship among a group of guys who had gone through every grade together. Together they blamed the outsider, Tony Reynard.

When Joey Ahearn, the deputy chief's boy, noticed the cruiser ambling over the tractor path from the firebreak, he started to back up toward his truck. "Of all the stupid stunts I've done! I can't believe I left the house again with all of you. I'm supposed to enlist next week. They won't want me with anything on my record!" If he could have run at that moment, he would have.

Claire made a harsh sound and took his arm. "Did you rape Sheri Lynn Baker, Joey?"

He shook his head, "Tony stopped us that night, but we knew what Nick Baker was doing. We did nothing to stop it from happening again." He looked down, "She had old bruises." Tears dripped down his face; he was the toughest of the gang of young punks that ran the town and surrounding county, "We didn't tell my father or anybody else. We made Tony keep quiet."

Claire's eyes were blurry with anger as she asked, "How?" Her eyes flashed dangerously toward Tony.

"We beat him up bad, and we all said the beating of little Rob was his doing," Sam spoke up as his tears fell.

Claire was furious. "You mean to tell me that Rob has spent the last week in the hospital, we have spent money on a lawyer, and Tony has lost his chances for a decent college disappear over keeping this quiet? It's a festering sore, boys. It will ruin your lives." There was a crack in her voice—harsh and stiff.

The deputy's cruiser had come to a stop, but Brian Reynard emerged instead of Deputy Hanson. Everyone looked horrified as he cocked the rifle and pointed it at Joey and Sam. "Let's have a moment of truth, boys, before I started blowing holes in people. Deputy Hanson is on his way to the hospital over all this."

Walt Stone finally came forward to intervene, "Mr. Reynard, put down the shotgun. Boys, walk back to our place, so Sarah and Julie can take the children back into the house. They don't need to hear all this. Let's get a written statement as soon as the state police arrive."

"But my dad," Joey started to interrupt after years of training to go to his father to cover up a number of blunders.

Walt shook his head and stated, "Your dad would be subject to investigation if he took the confessions of his son's best friends about an incident including his son. Have some sense!" He caught Claire's eye and smiled in that drugstore cowboy way that fooled most people. He walked right off the porch and took the gun from Brian.

Later after the state police left and the families of the assorted boys were on their way back to their homes, Sarah sat back in the kitchen chair and looked sharply at Brian Reynard. "Your sister says you have the makings of an accountant. I expected you to call me a month ago. I'll be blunt; tax season has started and I'm swamped. Interested in a crash course in tax preparation?" Brian looked up to see that Walt was grinning broadly. Walt Stone had captured a formidable woman when he married Sarah Monroe.

"Yes, thank you, Sarah. Thank you for talking to the boys today. Claire tells me you had them under control before the cavalry arrived." He grinned sheepishly.

She shrugged. "I just happened to be the calmest one on hand. See you at six this evening at my office in town. You know where it is?" He nodded, and she abruptly picked herself up and crossed to the backdoor. "Walt, I need a run before work."

"Okay, sweetheart." He watched her run out across the backyard with the pretty stone patio. Heedless of ice and snow, she bolted toward the track she'd worn into an old strawberry patch. Walt glanced back at Brian. "Good luck to you. Sarah will tell you straight out that it won't work if you mess up this opportunity. She doesn't talk like a woman when it comes to work. Not like your sister or even Gemma Stilton."

"Gemma is one of the strangest women I have ever met," Brian admitted and got up to watch with Walt as Sarah did her jogging laps to warm up.

"Well, you seem to bring it out then. I have never had a

problem talking to either woman, but that's me—a regular people person." Walt looked the other man in the eye. "You have designs on Gemma Stilton?"

"How could you know that?" Brian was shocked at Walt's bold question.

"Molly told us a story that featured a little boy named for your daddy—Luke—I think? Evidently you and Gemma are going to be parents very soon." Walt rubbed his whiskers and looked forward to shaving in the shower with his runaway girl who was blowing steam around the track like a racehorse.

Brian shook his head, but he smiled anyway. "That little girl is a good one for telling whoppers, but I wouldn't be too upset if it all worked out that way!" Both men watched Sarah run her worries around the track at the base of the mountain.

The day had given Sarah much to meditate about during her run. She had a little daughter to bring to womanhood on this farm, and she didn't want ugliness like she'd spied in the last twenty-four hours to touch her child. She didn't want it to touch any child; tears obscured her vision as she cleared her usual few miles to start her day on Lilac Hill. It was a good thing that she knew her way by feel alone.

5

Sheri Lynn Roberts was appalled at the person looking back at her in the mirror when she finally regained full consciousness later that day. Who was this purple-eyed, busted-up woman? Last she really checked, she had been a pretty blond in a tight waitress uniform serving pie to all the miners, truck drivers and salesmen who frequented the highway diner. It was a busy, truck stop diner near the crossroads between the interstate and the county roads. She'd been the belle of her shift: popular with the regulars, a flirt with new customers, and a favorite among full-time employees. She never turned down a shift if another waitress' kid was sick or there was a holiday. She could sub in for the short-order cook when they needed one which they often did because the full-time guy had a recurring problem with whiskey. That was before she married a man who wanted her to stay at home and promised to treat her like a princess.

Eighteen months ago, she had taken the job at the trucker's diner on the busy highway instead of suffering through slow tips at the Lambertville Diner. She had missed Claire and her old boss, but she'd been able to afford rent on the little single-wide trailer with her boyfriend who worked for the mine. He offered her a ring after another few months though she'd had to pay his part of the rent twice. A quick trip to the courthouse that year, and she was a married woman with hopes of a child on the way.

What a far cry from the throwaway girl she'd been in Wheeling. She wondered if her mother had worried for one moment about her middle child. Her dad had been gone for ten years—off to parts unknown. Hitching down to Lambertville had been a lark on her fifteenth birthday that let her pass herself off as eighteen and go to work full time.

The woman looking back in the mirror was finally eighteen, but she felt ninety.

Nick Baker had seemed like such a good guy, a white knight like Walt or one of his buddies like that Elliott man who was married to Juliet Monroe. Nick had put some mileage on her; that was for sure. Sheri Lynn glared at herself in the bathroom mirror and looked at the scars and bruises Nick had left like gifts on her skin. She thought about the crash they said he caused up the highway that killed him and Bobby yesterday. Good riddance, she mulled and shook her head.

What a waste of a life, she corrected and wondered how Bobby had gotten himself mixed up with Nick to start. She figured that Bobby had seen her in town talking to Tony Reynard, had seen the black eye and the busted lips, and assumed she'd been hurt by the boy. She ran a vicious brush through her knotted hair. In another life, Tony Reynard might have been her high school boyfriend, but in this one, he was just some heroic kid who spoke up for her instead of raping her like the other guys did. Nick Baker had been a sick man, and she had fallen for his promises.

She blew out another breath that she held to keep from crying out as the brush jammed up again in the knots left by the last vicious attack. At least it had only been Nick this time in frenzy from cocaine she watched him snort. She thought he might kill her before he cut the ropes he'd used and demanded dinner served in ten minutes. His eyes had been wild and rolled around out of control. She had managed not to cry or scream during the attack by saying the "Our Father" over and over again in her head. Even when she lapsed into sleep last night, the words repeated in her mind.

"Hallowed be thy name," she said aloud to her reflection and frowned. Now that Nick was dead, maybe she could go back to her other name and forget the last three years. Maybe she could go back to being eighteen instead of her alias, a worn-out and abused, twenty-one-year-old widow.

The state police picked up the woman they thought was Sheri Lynn Roberts for questioning after they searched the trailer with her name on the lease. The dead girl tied in her place on the dirty bed turned out to be a prostitute from the Wheeling area who was only sixteen. Evidently, Nick liked his ladies to be young and unfettered by relatives or friends to check up on them.

In the process of examining the dead man's effects, the identification for an Eve Briton had been found. The Briton girl was a missing person from three years ago, so dogs had been brought in to search the woods and crawlspace under the trailer.

Gemma Stilton had rushed into the barracks after getting Sheri Lynn's message that the trooper's had taken her in for questioning. Claire had been elbows deep in preparations for a large company dinner party, and the Monroe girls were both at work. Gemma considered calling Eben to suggest a lawyer the moment she heard the accusatory tone of the trooper's interview.

Gemma Stilton groaned inwardly when Sheri's eyes bugged out at the mention of a missing person. She watched the woman's cheeks go scarlet, and her fingers begin to tremble. Gemma leaned forward and whispered, "You tell them the truth right now. I knew you were a liar the moment I met you last night! Thank God you weren't lying about the attack. If that poor deputy has been shot in front of me because you lied about that, I might beat you myself."

The state policeman doing the interview stood over the two women fearing that a fight might occur. They were bristling at each other like a pair of cats.

Sheri shook her head and hissed at Gemma, "Okay, okay, spooky Stilton. You don't scare me with the ridiculous second sight mumbo jumbo." She glared at the older woman who looked like a witch right out of a Halloween story with her claws extended.

The officer crooked an eyebrow at their tense conversation, but he sat back down when both women sighed simultaneously. Sheri leaned forward and admitted, "I am Eve Briton. That missing girl is me," she gulped, "or was me three years ago. I ran off the day I turned fifteen—everybody forgot my birthday: my mother, brothers, teachers and friends. Nobody said one word. Sad sack that I was and mad at the world, I hitched a ride south and landed in Lambertville. I had a fake ID and started working with a made up social. I was doing just fine until I fell for Nick Baker." Her throat closed up imagining the wreck near the diner that killed him and Bobby.

The trooper raised a brow but nodded. "We'll fingerprint you and compare it to the FBI database. It would be a sorry thing to be charged as an accessory to your own murder if your claim is true. That Reynard boy is the only reason you aren't facing charges for the murder of the other girl. You were seen with Reynard yesterday in town hours before she was picked up in Wheeling. According to the Reynard family, you were with one or another Reynard or Spence from that time nonstop. This is an abduction, assault and murder case,

Ms. Baker . . . or Briton. Do you think we will find any other bodies?"

Sheri shook her head in utter shock, "Lord, I hope not! Bad enough he kept me like a prisoner on the place, but I hope he just hurt me. He was nice at first. I didn't even know about the drugs until we were married. Then I was stuck. What a terrible man!"

Gemma turned gentler as the woman beside her shrank into violent memories. Reaching over, Gemma took one of the hands that were twisting together on her lap. "Eve?" She smiled at the startled look the younger woman gave her, "You are going to put Sheri Lynn out of your mind and return to Eve Briton. I know you didn't do anything except hurt yourself. They won't find anything else at your place. You must start over today for the baby's sake." She patted Eve's hand and nodded at the shocked policeman.

6

Walt Stone grinned at his little girl's wobbling masterpiece of pastry dough and jelly as she served it with a bit of her mother's jaunty flourish. "Oh, Megan! What a fine . . ." he gulped for one moment. One day is was pie, another it was a truffle, yesterday the concoction had been a croissant said in such a way he could never duplicate the word.

"Tart! An apricot tart!" the disembodied voice of Sarah was echoed immediately by his precious three-year-old. Little Megan's grin was just like his, but her eyes were all Sarah.

"Thank you, sweetheart!" he ate the teetering mass without inspecting it like he might have in the past. The querulous Megan ruled the roost, but his darling wife rarely let anything suspect leave the kitchen. He hummed and gave his review that often sent him to the thesaurus to find yet another way to praise pastry dough. "Scrumptious filling with light, flaky layers—excellent tart, my darling."

He wiggled his eyebrows to delight her into giggles. He was amazed that even three-year-old girls enjoyed his down home shtick as much as the older ones did.

Sarah leaned on the doorway and smiled at her goofy husband, "You're a scrumptious man, Walt Stone. Such a great daddy!" She sailed across the floor with her arms wide to make her daughter giggle even more before coming in for a landing on her husband's lap. She kissed him as his hands rose to touch her rounding abdomen. They looked into each other's eyes and smiled. Such was harmony in Lavender Cottage of Monroe Farm on Lilac Hill.

Gemma Reynard was having a tough time justifying her quick marriage to the caustic and overwhelmingly domineering Brian Reynard just in time for dinner. "Where did you go after work, Gemma?" Brian was waiting with hand on hip while their dinner waited in the oven and going dry in his mind.

She huffed a moment and then grouched it out in a way that erased all time off purgatory for her kind act. "I drove Eve up to Wheeling to see her mama. The old lady's sick and has been begging the girl to visit." She flounced in on a wave of hormones so thick, she didn't see her husband wince.

At the dining room table, Molly chuckled while she colored. This love affair between her mother and Brian Reynard had not been a smooth one to navigate, but it had been interesting. They might argue, but they were building toward some greater understanding.

"Slip off your shoes and wash up. I'll put dinner on the table, and you can tell about your adventures with the gimmes." He rolled his eyes and turned away.

Gemma followed him into the kitchen indignant. "I am supposed to be the intuitive one, not you! How about the next time you tell me before I drive a two-hour round trip just to break the girl's heart?" She kicked off her shoes and washed both hands and face in the kitchen sink.

Brian laughed, "So we're calling it 'intuition' now instead of second sight or just plain old telepathy! It doesn't take much to figure out a con game Eve's mother might cook up after the publicity that Lambertville got from the Nick Baker story. Bet the woman was a user," he turned Gemma to face him with his one hand at her waist. Sometimes he wished for another arm to hold her very tight, so she could feel safe.

Gemma nodded with exhausted tears in her eyes. "She hit Eve up for five thousand dollars thinking there would be some big insurance policy. Eve looked like she'd just been slapped. We left immediately." The baby flutter-kicked, so she moved his hand to the spot and leaned against his chest briefly. "That's your boy in there making himself known. Another numbers man, I think."

Molly joined them to touch the spot where the baby reached for the outside. She opened her palm and summoned the child to her touch. She smiled as he brushed by like a slumbering giant. "A scientist. I think." She looked up into her mother's green eyes and grouched, "He doesn't see like we do." It sobered her.

Gemma smiled at her daughter's pout. "Well, that's a good thing. Can you imagine a numbers man like Brian glimpsing the future and seeing pieces of the past? It will all be good."

Molly nodded, "Miss Eve is satisfied about her mother and brothers. She knows they are well and haven't changed. She wouldn't be ready for the next step if you hadn't taken her today." She glanced up to Brian who was enraptured with the taps and nudges from his unborn son. She smiled at her step-father, "Could we eat? I'm starving!"

Eve Briton worked the late shift for the catering crew with Claire Spence. The fancy party for some visiting politician extended from the dining room to the sunroom at the Lambert Mansion. As Reynard Catering, they'd readied twenty-five trays of canapés and drinks for the esteemed guest list. Eve felt the sudden urge to peek out into the throng though she was working food prep with the kitchen crew.

Later Eve would tell herself that she'd heard his voice and recognized it. Standing with a drink in a small knot of people, the familiar man was lit by some unseen spotlight so that his hair glinted golden and his skin glowed with a deeper tan than he'd had when she'd last seen him. Perhaps he'd been away for a while, she thought and wondered if he'd recognize her now.

She had let her hair grow back in her natural, darker blond, and her face had lost that gaunt hollowness from frequent abuse. Eve felt healthier than she ever had in her life as the baby grew beneath her taut belly. At six months, she was barely into maternity clothes where Claire at only five months bloomed with loose shirts and flowing, light layers. Eben often joked that he felt buoyed by the waves of estrogen in his big house on Lilac Hill.

The blond-haired man was talking to Jason Lambert and standing beside a beautiful redhead who looked vaguely familiar. Eve wondered if they were married and hoped it wasn't true. She could only remember their moments of joining in her bed and then how his eyes had filled with tears when he realized her drugged condition. There might have been angry words with Nick before he left. She wondered what sort of man he was and worried about the nature of the little being growing inside her. She wanted to know his name for the child's sake. She wanted to know what sort of man he might be. She picked up a tray without thinking and swept into the great room to circulate right into his path.

Eve overheard Jason Lambert address the man as "Richard," but she mentally labeled him "dick" with a small smirk. The three waved away her tray as Mr. Lambert caught her giving the man a searching look. Lambert pumped the man for any extra information he could gather. He didn't have to be clairvoyant to notice Eve Briton's interest.

Jason left the redhead with the Richard character after a few more minutes asking questions that bordered on impolite. He had watched Eve try to avoid dumping an entire tray of cheese, crackers and miniature quiche on his guests. Sleuthing for information evidently disrupted her usual polished glide through the dining room they'd opened to the solarium for the crowd. She was so young, he mused, as she stumbled over explaining the contents of the tray to the mayor. This woman Eve was younger than his Sarah had been when she disrupted his life so completely a few years ago. This young woman threatened to upset anyone she touched with her lurid past, hidden identity and open curiosity about one of his guests.

He gestured to her and then led her right back into the kitchen where the head chef Maggie and Claire were rushing through dessert preparations. "Miss Briton? Why were you out there scoping out the crowd?"

Eve blinked at the big boss's sharp eyes but shrugged without any embarrassment, "That man Richard looks like someone I've met." She blushed just enough and glanced toward Claire for help.

Claire raised a brow but said nothing. She was in awe of Jason Lambert. His appearance in the kitchen during a catered party was unusual. Though Sarah Monroe teased with the big man, he ran a research lab that brought visitors from all over the east coast to their little valley town. Few people could boast that they were easy with him. Usually he was a quiet, impassive shadow at the town meetings, church services or some Lambert-sponsored event in town. Even the hijinks of his recent marriage hadn't made him approachable.

She looked to Miss Maggie, the head cook and undisputed ruler of the staff in the big house and lab that comprised the Lambert farm, mansion, gardens and Lilac Hill Research. Miss Maggie would wave them all out of the kitchen if she sensed disruption.

Maggie Turner screwed her mouth up as if she tasted something sour, "Eve Briton, what do you want to know about that man you noticed an hour ago? Then go back to filling these shells; they're due out in five minutes." She wiped a hand on her apron and glared at both Eve and Jason. The old woman was gruff with pretended aggravation, "Jason, you know better than to come into my kitchen more than once a day to aggravate the staff." She rolled her eyes and smirked.

That morning he had visited under the pretense of

filching early coffee and a sweet roll from Sarah Monroe and had finished with her in tears yet again. But after he left the room, Sarah had burst into unusual giggles and refused to share the secret she and her half-brother had shared. Later Maggie caught her glancing through a binder of cakes that she'd made for the Lamberts during her three-year career as their pastry chef.

Jason grinned at Maggie which creased the old scars on the left side of his face and revealed their contours. "Yes, ma'am."

He turned to Eve who had picked up the large cream tube with slightly shaky fingers. "His name is Richard Galenburg. He runs a small firm in Richmond that brokers repurposed equipment for the mine where your husband worked. That's how you know him. Let's see..." He rolled his eyes upward and recited, "Divorced for a few years and two children. Lives with his parents right now because his dad had a heart attack a few months back and underwent major heart surgery." He grinned again with a facial expression that could have been interpreted as malicious in the unkind, overhead lighting. "How'd I do?"

Eve quavered over a smile. "Thank you, Mr. Lambert. You're quite . . . intuitive for a man." She blushed, trembled and inadvertently squirted a dollop of cream filling on the floor. Maggie and Claire glared at both of them.

Jason rocked back on his heels as Maggie began to growl the word, "Out!"

He turned and exited muttering something like "seems I haven't lost my touch" in obvious enjoyment. He was whistling as he exited and crossed the dining room toward the redhead who continued to speak to Galenburg.

Eve turned to Maggie, who threw her a towel to mop up the hazardous cream slick on the floor. "Men are odd things, aren't they, Miss Maggie?"

Maggie smirked. "The girl is learning! At least he doesn't make you cry." With an eyebrow arched upward, the old woman imperiously waved them all back to work.

Eve shook her head and thought through all the

information that Jason Lambert had given her about the baby's father. Galenburg had to be some other user fiend under that golden boy appearance. She unwittingly rested a hand on her slightly protruding belly and let her mouth settle into a thinking frown. She wondered who the pretty redhead might be. She glanced out to the crowd and let herself worry over some other woman for a change.

About The Author

Joan D. Cooper moved to Maryland's Eastern Shore ten years ago and shifted from writing poetry to spinning fiction. A career educator, she finds inspiration in her three children, extended family, lifelong friends and two rambunctious dogs. Member of the *Eastern Shore Writer's Association*, advisor for *Poetry Out Loud* and patron of Brown Box Theatre Project's *Free Shakespeare at the Beach* initiative, she is committed to teaching and writing.

Contact her at www.joandcooper.com for other projects and a creative writing blog.

Sarah Monroe's tale of mystery and romance begins in *Finding Home on Lilac Hill.*